Hilton Headings

Island Writers' Network
Hilton Head Island, SC

Hilton Headings

Edited by:

Margaret Lorine
Sansing McPherson
Jane Hill
Norma Van Amberg

Island Writers' Network
Hilton Head Island, SC

Copyright © 2009

Many selections included in this anthology are works of fiction. Except for historical figures, places and events, all characters and their actions in these stories are products of the authors' imaginations. Other selections are based on the authors' own experiences or research.

Front cover photograph by Sansing McPherson, used with permission. Pelican insert courtesy of the National Park Service, www.nps.gov.

Cover design by David Russell; interior layout by Jane P. Hill.

This project is partially funded through a grant from the Arts Council of Beaufort County with funds from the City of Beaufort and SC Arts Commission through the NEA. Additional funding is from the John & Susan Bennett Memorial Arts Fund of the Coastal Community Foundation of SC.

A project of:

The Island Writers' Network
P. O. Box 5039
Hilton Head Island, SC 29938
www.iwn-hhi.org

Published by

Catawba Publishing Company
Charlotte, NC
www.catawbapublishing.com

ISBN 978-1-59712-381-5

Printed in the United States of America

First Printing

Table of Contents

Hello, Honey... 1
by James Edward Alexander
The Hamper... 3
by Tom Crawford
Invisible Fences..................................... 7
by Sansing McPherson
Solitude... 19
by Sharon Rice
Picker Singin' on the Step........................... 20
by Marilyn Lorenz
Mountaintop Experiences: Lowcountry Ribs..... 21
by Max D. Judge
Butterfly Man.. 25
by Raymond P. Berberian
Double Coupons...................................... 33
by Norm Levy
From the Skeleton of Her Story..................... 34
by Frederick W. Bassett
White Egret.. 35
by Bob Hamel
A Gator Can Hope.................................... 37
by Will Anderson
Old Ford... 42
by Art Cornell
Good Dog.. 43
by Bobbi Hahn
No-See-Ums.. 46
by Greg Smorol
Earth Day, Every Day................................ 48
by Bob Hamel
The Legend of Clipper Gates......................... 49
by Len Camarda
Grandmother... 60
by Marilyn Lorenz

Learning from Mice..................................... 61
    by Charlie McOuat
An Unspoken Promise................................. 65
    by Greg Smorol
Tit for Tat.. 70
    by Norm Levy
The Blind Leading the Blind: Two Navigators... 71
    by James Edward Alexander
Preserving and Protecting Hilton Head Island... 77
    by Norma Van Amberg
Night Winds... 81
    by Max D. Judge
Mother Moon.. 82
    by Sharon Rice
Eve's Revenge... 83
    by Sheila Gale
North toward Home.................................... 90
    by Frederick W. Bassett
Fickle.. 91
    by Art Cornell
Striving.. 91
    by Art Cornell
Poems Written While in Japan....................... 92
    by Norm Levy
Pauline.. 94
    by Sharon Rice
Lobster Love... 95
    by Charlie McOuat
The Tryst... 107
    by C. S. Thorn, Jr.
Crows.. 116
    by Frederick W. Bassett
Funny Money.. 118
    by Norm Levy
A Scent of Lilac... 119
    by Sharon Rice
Realization... 126
    by Marilyn Lorenz
Home of the Brave..................................... 127
    by Bobbi Hahn

Homemade Fig Preserves............................ 129
by Frederick W. Bassett
Hands.. 130
by Art Cornell
Henry's Diet.. 131
by Jim Van Cleave
Season's Change..................................... 141
by Art Cornell
Storm.. 141
by Art Cornell
The Old Enmity...................................... 142
by Frederick W. Bassett
The Gifts of an Addicted Daughter................ 144
by Marilyn Lorenz
Midnight Requisitioning............................ 145
by James Edward Alexander
A Lid Slipped down over the Eye.................. 148
by Sharon Rice
Autumn Fading....................................... 150
by Bob Hamel
A True Confederate................................. 151
by Greg Smorol
Prayer for My Grandson............................. 158
by Marilyn Lorenz
Cottageville.. 159
by Tom Crawford
The Beachcomber.................................... 163
by Shanti North
The Busy People..................................... 172
by Bobbi Hahn
Control.. 174
by Art Cornell
Bouquet... 174
by Art Cornell
The World of Golf................................... 175
by Dee Merian

Max... 181
    by Bobbi Hahn
Maple Creek Bridge...................................... 183
    by Sharon Rice
Coffee Shop on Fourth Street........................ 184
    by Sharon Rice
Love Affair at the Beach............................... 185
    by Anne Grace
The Bardo of Living and Dying...................... 187
    by Margaret Lorine

Table of
Photographs and Illustrations

Live Oak.. 6
Photograph by Sansing McPherson
Coastline in the Mist................................. 19
From a photograph by Art Cornell
Monarch... 24
Photograph by Sansing McPherson
White Egret... 35
From a photograph by Art Cornell
Ali Gator.. 36
Drawing by Jane Anderson
Santee Cooper Swamp............................. 64
Photograph by Jane Hill
Shrimp Boat... 76
Photograph by Bobbi Hahn
Shelter Cove Community Park.................... 80
Photograph by Norma Van Amberg
Dancers' Silhouette.................................. 81
Illustration by Ann Judge-Wegener
Daffodils.. 91
From a watercolor by Jane Hill
Osprey.. 99
Photograph by Sansing McPherson
Hilton Head Sunset.................................. 100
Photograph by Art Cornell
Saw Palmetto.. 101
Photograph by Sansing McPherson
Egret.. 102
Photograph by Linda Benning
Baby Alligator.. 103
Photograph by Sansing McPherson
Kayakers... 104
Photograph by Art Cornell

Shrimp Boats.. 105
    Photograph by Roger Benning
Sunrise over Port Royal Sound.................... 106
    Photograph by Sansing McPherson
Storm Clouds.. 141
    From photograph by Art Cornell
Field of Wildflowers at Sea Pines................. 158
    Photograph by Sansing McPherson
Collector's Red Sox Tag............................ 161
    Photograph by Phyllis Crawford
Driftwood Tree.. 162
    Photograph by Bobbi Hahn
Hydrangeas.. 174
    From a watercolor by Jane Hill

Hello, Honey

by
James Edward Alexander

Some days I spend a few fleeting seconds with a special lady of my childhood. Her spirit visits me by invitation when I sometimes close my eyes and imagine her outstretched arms welcoming me to a momentary cradle of comfort. When I recognize the lingering smell of Octagon soap on the hands of a wash woman, her emanation is confirmed.

Her name was Melissa, a name as lyrical as my vision of her. Miss Melissa was an old lady whose face was as black as the tar on the edge of the highway, where she waited each morning to greet us on our way to school during the decade 1935 to 1945. Her presence was as certain as the steeple on the church three doors from her front step. On those cold days as we walked to school, we needed that assurance.

Each child received the same salutation, "Hello, honey," and a smile that warmed us from our forehead to our feet. Then she embraced each of us, and something unusual happened. Within that brief close encounter Miss Melissa's agile fingers re-did each child. She re-buttoned, re-wrapped, and re-positioned hats and gloves with such speed and deftness that seemed magical. Despite her old age, her nimble fingers moved so adroitly as to suggest that her greeting and care were her sole purposes in life. Having been re-done, we positioned ourselves for her gentle valediction, a warm kiss on the cheek.

Now, in my reverie, I hear, "Hello, honey," and I open my eyes. My time is up. There is a long line behind me.

James Edward Alexander, lives in Bluffton, SC, and writes stories of a happy childhood in Valdosta, GA. More stories are shared in his book, *Half Way Home From Kinderlou.*

The Hamper

by
Tom Crawford

The decision by the Piggly Wiggly grocery chain to stop offering Green Stamps to its customers provoked a withdrawal from my memory bank.

The Associated Press report on the Piggly Wiggly action at its store in Columbia, Tennessee, was carried in the *Telegram and Gazette* of Worcester, Massachusetts, on February 15, 2003. I clipped it for sentimental reasons—memories linking my shopping nearly fifty years ago with my current shopping at the Piggly Wiggly in Coligny Plaza on Hilton Head Island.

I had not realized that S&H Green Stamps was based in Salem, Massachusetts, and that the promotion was founded in 1896. During its heyday in the 1960s, Green Stamps penetrated sixty percent of American households. At that time, S&H was the largest purchaser of consumer products in the world. But I could certainly accept those facts, having been in that majority.

Our family—two adults, one infant son, and seven-ninths of a daughter—flew from Amsterdam to Boston in August of 1960. We had brought only 110 pounds of personal property with us to establish our new home in Springfield, Massachusetts, where I had been assigned as bureau manager for United Press International. Several months later, with the assistance of family, friends, and new colleagues, we had most of the basic needs for the new household,

But among the things still missing was a hamper.

We decided that the Green Stamps we were collecting from the A&P supermarket on State Street in Springfield, opposite the then still-booming Springfield Armory, would be directed toward a hamper.

Finally the big day arrived. I headed toward State Street to the S&H redemption center just up a block from the A&P. Unfortunately it was a Saturday, and lines were long. There was a line to obtain merchandise and another shorter one for exchanges or errors. It took the better part of an hour to get to the counter in Line Number One, but the clerk was efficient and polite. She noted my selection and quickly returned from the back warehouse with our new hamper.

On my return home I headed straight for the bathroom to deposit the week's dirty laundry in the new hamper. I then returned to the kitchen for a well-deserved cup of coffee.

Only then did my wife discover my folly. She examined the hamper and determined that I had been hoodwinked. I had brought home the seven-book hamper and had yielded nine books of Green Stamps for it. She was adamant and I repentant.

I swiftly checked the catalogue and established that I had indeed sacrificed nine books of stamps for a seven-book hamper. Contritely, I headed back to the center.

Apparently I was not the only miscreant or victim of clerical error. The first line was now much shorter than the second, and it took almost a half-hour to get back to the desk.

Embarrassed, I explained what had happened, and I asked the clerk to confirm that we had indeed been short-changed—that I had yielded nine books of stamps for a seven-book hamper. I held the hamper up as proof.

The clerk disappeared quickly into the labyrinth, catalogue in hand, and soon returned with the nine-book hamper. The exchange was made, and it was back home to Federal Street.

This time, the wife was waiting to confirm that the correct transaction had been completed. She seized the nine-book hamper, headed for the bathroom, and soon returned with an exasperated look on her face.

"Where's the dirty laundry?" she asked.

There were several people still on duty when I arrived for my third visit to the redemption center, not long before closing time. A new clerk finally agreed to allow me to survey the hampers in the warehouse in her presence to establish both my veracity and my eccentricity.

We finally found the original seven-book hamper; and on flipping open the top, there, lo and behold, lay the Crawford family's dirty laundry. I transferred it to a laundry bag I had brought for the purpose, and I slipped out of the S&H Green Stamp center as unobtrusively as possible.

Live Oak

Photograph by Sansing McPherson

Invisible Fences

by
Sansing McPherson

Amy knew Baker had it in for them from day one, starting with the tape on the trees.

She and Joe had taken the kids to see their lot the day of the tree survey. As their car approached, an older man stood in the yard next door, staring at their property. The mailbox name read *Baker*. Joe lowered the window to speak, but the man turned abruptly and went into his house.

"Friendly sort," Joe said as he parked the car.

"Why'd you say that for?" six-year-old Josie asked from the back seat. "He didn't seem friendly to me."

"It's sarcasm, stupid," said eight-year-old Connor. Josie stuck out her tongue at him. In her pink ballet leotard she looked like a mischievous pixie. Connor wore all black, including cape and boots. He bolted from the car, found a stick, and began fencing with a sweet gum sapling.

"Slay those mosquitoes, Zorro," Joe called.

Amy gazed at the leafy expanse that would shade their new home from the Lowcountry sun. Her heart lurched when she saw red tape around the trunk of a sprawling live oak. Was it dead meat for bulldozers? She looked for the surveyor. Josie was already talking to him.

"Why do some trees have blue ribbons and some have red and some have green?" she chirped. "Why didn't you use pink ribbons, like my dance costume?" She ended with a pirouette that spun her little dance skirt out from her bird-like legs.

"The trees with red are the ones they have to cut down," pronounced Connor.

"Actually," the surveyor said, "I tape each tree as I measure and record it with whatever color I happen to grab. Despite what most people think, the colors don't mean a thing."

"Nya-a, Connor. You don't know everything." Josie smirked.

Relieved that her oak was safe, Amy noticed the surveyor had used green tape on the south side of the lot, switched to red in the center, and ended with blue on the pines by the unfriendly neighbor's property.

The man dug a small roll of pink tape from his pocket and offered it to Josie. She thanked him and turned to leer at Connor. Amy snapped digital photos of their lot with its beribboned trees to document this early step in the building of their dream home.

They had decided on a gated community after years of noisy neighbors in an ungated area. On one side Motorcycle Michael rebuilt Harleys in his garage nights and weekends. On the other side a sixteen-year-old played Death Rock on his amped-up car radio whenever he washed his Firebird. They learned teenage boys wash cars as often as teenage girls wash hair.

Then there was the bullying. Biker Mike's ten-year-old son did not understand Connor's penchant for fantasy games. He mocked Connor's costumes and broke his plastic Excalibur sword. Then they found Connor's Clone Trooper helmet smashed on the front step with "Death to Wusses" scrawled on it in red. Connor stopped playing outside. He withdrew into his books, taking his gloom out on Josie, who became a fast draw at ratting on her brother.

The new house brought hope. Gated plantations had covenants, and people respected them, right?

When their lot was excavated, they returned to check the progress. The grand live oak stood in an ideal spot of what would become their front yard. Amy took picture after picture of the site before noticing the line of pines next to Baker's yard. They had red tape around them.

Odd, she thought. *I know that tape was blue last week.*

Was she crazy for remembering wrong, or was she crazy for needing to prove herself right? She reviewed the earlier shots on the camera's digital display. Sure enough, the pines were tagged in blue.

A workman loading tools into his truck solved the mystery.

"Y'all got an awfully meddlesome neighbor." He nodded toward Baker's house. "He kept insisting we were supposed to take out them pines."

Amy and Joe exchanged looks. Their dream home was not coming with a dream neighbor.

As building progressed, they visited almost daily. Whenever they saw Baker, he found a weed to pull on the opposite side of his property or disappeared entirely.

The Caines across the street came over to meet them and said they had never conversed much with Baker. All they knew was that his name was David; they rarely saw his wife, Lydia; and he was a stickler about covenants.

"We call him the Covenant Nazi," Hal Caine said. "He once called the POA because I left a ladder out for two days." Hal suggested planting a wax myrtle hedge laced with poison ivy and ignoring him.

On moving day the van had not been in front of their house twenty minutes before a plantation security cruiser pulled into their drive. An officer got out, introduced herself politely as Merritt, and consulted with the movers. Amy and Joe watched a rapid conversation involving much gesturing toward the van, glances at Baker's house, and a final shrug from Merritt before she drove away.

"Is somebody getting arrested?" Connor yelled from an upstairs window where he and Josie were watching a DVD.

"Not yet," said Joe. "Finish your movie. We'll call you when it's time to leave for jail."

They heard Josie's voice squeak, "Jail?" and Connor's retort, "Sarcasm."

"Y'all shore got a ornery neighbor," the head mover said, rolling a hand truck up the driveway. "He told security we're encroachin' on his property. Heck, it's a public street."

Stung by the complaint, Amy's energy sagged. Boxes grew heavier. Packing tape defied scissors. She threw bubble wrap onto the kitchen floor with an attitude. She had just spilled an entire box of silverware when the doorbell rang. Picturing Baker there with another complaint, she crawled under the round oak breakfast table to retrieve a spoon and stayed there.

"It's open," she hollered irritably.

Dottie Caine came in bearing sandwiches and sweet tea. She bent down with a quizzical grin at a crouching Amy.

"I thought you were Baker," Amy explained. "He's already called Security."

Dottie gave a sympathetic hand up and invited them for wine that evening.

A week later Amy and Joe were building a rose bed on the sunny side of the driveway by the pines. Standing to ease their backs, they came face to face with Baker shouldering a rake like a rifle.

"I gotta say it's a hell of a lot quieter now without that construction racket."

"Mr. Baker, isn't it?" said Joe, pulling off a work glove and extending his hand. "I'm Joe Beck, and this is Amy."

Baker ignored the hand. "You screwed up not taking out the pines when you had the big equipment here. It'll cost you a damn sight more and cause another hellacious ruckus to cut them down later."

"We like the pines," Joe said mildly.

"Trash trees," snapped Baker. "They drop needles and cones, and they're the first thing to go flying in a storm. Guided missiles, right through your window. They shade my yard so I can't grow grass, and the wife never could grow roses."

"Doesn't the plantation require a permit to take out trees?" Amy asked.

"You already blew your best chance," said Baker, flapping a dismissive arm toward them and turning away.

It did not help that Joe, adjusting a pop-up irrigation sprinkler, sprayed Baker as he pruned azaleas.

It did not help when they got the new puppy, either. Gypsy was five months old, and the little gray fluff ball lived up to her name by sneaking out any half-cracked door and roaming into neighboring yards.

Dottie Caine brought Gypsy back one day, the escape artist joyfully licking her face.

"I turned around in my kitchen," said Dottie, "and there was Gypsy, on her back, begging for a tummy scratch."

It seemed cute until Amy heard Baker shouting profanities at the pup a day later.

One afternoon Amy answered the doorbell to find Baker on her front porch, clutching Gypsy under his arm.

"Don't you know how to live in a gated community?" he said, squeezing the wriggling puppy tighter. "We have a leash law."

"I know. I'm sorry. She just slipped out." Amy replied, taking Gypsy from him.

"And we have a pooper scooper law." Baker took a plastic bucket from behind his back and deposited dog poop on the porch.

Still trembling, Amy told Joe and concluded, "The covenants forbid fences. With the kids coming and going, we'll never stop her. Let's try an invisible fence."

"Would it work on Baker?" Joe asked.

Connor had a fantasy field day with the invisible fence concept. He stood at the end of the driveway with wizard's cloak and wand yelling "Zap!" whenever Gypsy ventured toward the street. With her electronic collar, Gypsy soon learned the property boundaries. She also cowered under the table whenever Connor picked up the wand.

One late July day Connor and Josie were enjoying a rare détente playing Super Heroes in the branches of the live oak. A fluffy white dog came into the yard, prompting barks from Gypsy and a wail of dismay from Josie that the invisible fence did not keep the other dog out. Moments later a slender girl came out Baker's door calling the name Mookie. The intruding dog ignored her as he and Gypsy sniffed each other and began romping under the oak. The girl spied Mookie and strode unabashedly into the yard.

Connor dropped easily from the tree. Legs apart and arms folded over his Superman tee shirt, he stared at the girl. Josie scrambled down beside him.

"This your dog?" Connor challenged.

"Yeah. He got away."

"So who are you?" Josie asked

"I'm Rona. My mom and I are visiting Gramma and Grampa."

"How old are you?" Connor asked, eyeing her from head to toe.

"Seven. I'm going into second grade."

"I'm going into third," said Connor, mustering all his arrogance.

"So why do you still wear Underoos?" Rona scoffed.

Connor blushed crimson. "It's a costume, stupid."

"Was that sarcasm, Connor?" Josie asked, but he stalked into the house without reply. Josie turned back to Rona and said, "Wanna walk dogs?"

Thus the girls began a daily ritual. Connor moped alone until Amy discovered the local youth theater had an opening at their final camp session.

"Rona says she and her mom might hafta move here 'cause her Gramma's sick," Josie told her mother one day as they weeded the rose bed. "Rona says she's got *all* shiners."

Amy looked at Baker's shady yard and recalled her first conversation with him. "*. . . the wife never could grow roses.*" Guilt descended. She stared at her own fetal rosebushes, full of buds but not blooms.

Grow, dammit!

A week before school started, five roses opened. Gathering the nerve to take them over to Baker's and ring that doorbell, her courage dissolved when the front door flew open and Baker's curses propelled Mookie out to seek refuge under the oak.

"What did he do?" Amy asked when Rona came to fetch him.

"Pooped on the rug. I sure hope we don't hafta move here."

"It must be hard to have your grandma sick."

"Yeah," said Rona, digging a toe into the sandy earth under the oak. "She won't let Mom or Grampa out of her sight, or she cries that they're leaving her."

Amy fought back tears. "Can I take some roses to your grandma?"

"I don't think anybody oughta go in that house until Mom cleans the carpet."

"Has your granddad thought about finding someplace to care for your grandma?"

"No. When Mom suggested it, he said Gramma stood by him through his cancer; and she stood by Mom when my dad left us, so we hafta stand by her."

If Josie had not bounded out of the house with Gypsy just then, Amy would have wept. Later, when Rona started home, Amy clipped the roses and sent them over with her.

Just before school began, Rona announced she and her mother were going home. Amy felt relief for Rona, but Josie wailed that she was losing her very best friend ever.

The girls met for one final day together. Amy had bought a small album for Rona and inserted pictures of the girls and dogs. She grilled Josie's favorite petite hamburgers for lunch and served them under the oak.

Growls and screeches brought Amy back outside sooner than she expected.

"Mookie stole my Baby Burger," Josie shrieked. "And he bit Gypsy. He bit her!"

"You shouldn't have turned your back," Rona retorted.

"He's a big fat Super Pig," Josie screamed.

"They were just snotty booger burgers," taunted Rona.

"You're the snotty booger burger."

"I'm glad I'm leaving. Here's your stupid album. I don't ever want to see your stupid face again." Rona threw the book at Josie, grazing the top of her head.

Josie yowled, her tiny tongue quivering, the veins and tendons in her neck stretched taut as guy wires. Rona and Mookie stomped home.

"I hate her; I hate her," Josie sobbed into her mother's shoulder. "And she was my best friend." Her little frame shook with heartbreak.

Once school started and Josie reconnected with friends from kindergarten, tranquility returned. Connor continued with the youth theater and reveled in the costume opportunities. Even the hurricane season was kind to the East Coast. Until one evening in mid-September. A tropical depression strengthened offshore, accompanied by torrential rains. Through the kitchen window they watched storm-tossed trees and webs of lightning crackling across the sky.

Suddenly a concussive shock hit the house, overwhelming all senses—deafening thunder; instant darkness; shattering glass; a rush of humid air; the odors of ozone and burned pitch; and through it all, Josie's piercing shriek. Joe found a flashlight and checked for damages.

"Holy moley!" he exclaimed as the beam illuminated the dining room. Amy and the kids scuttled up behind him. A tree penetrated the window, its claw-like branches raking the dining table.

"There's broken glass," he warned. "Take the kids upstairs while I check things out."

From the upstairs window they saw by a lightning flash that one of their pines had splintered part-way down. The broken trunk lay across their driveway, its end impaling the dining room window.

Baker's prophecy, thought Amy.

As fast as the storm began, it exited northward. Hal Caine came over with heavy plastic, and by the headlights from his car he and Joe secured the gaping hole as best they could with the tree stuck in it.

Huddled together in Amy and Joe's bed, the kids eventually fell asleep. Not so their parents. At first light they assessed damages. Besides shattering the window, the intruding tree had cracked the cherry dining table that had been Amy's grandmother's. Two adjacent pines were scorched and split. The roses were fried. Hal brought his chain saw over before seven and began buzzing away at the fallen pine.

A security officer arrived. "Noise covenant," he apologized. "Can it wait until eight? We had a complaint."

They managed to get the kids off to school. By noon, when power was restored, they had contacted their insurance broker, ordered a replacement window, found a furniture repairman, and hired an arborist. Three pines had to come down. Amy fretted at the irony that Baker was getting his wish at their expense. She had nightmares of him lunging into their dining room window with his rake. Finally, with the window replaced and the trees removed, only the gap in the pines and the missing table reminded them of the ordeal.

Then one night they awoke to sirens and red and blue lights flashing on the bedroom ceiling. Pulling on clothes, they went to the door to see an ambulance in Baker's driveway and EMTs bringing out a figure strapped to a gurney. Dead or alive? They could not tell. Another medic emerged, assisting a limping Baker down the steps. Joe sprinted over to offer help.

Upon return he said, "I'm going to sit with Baker in the ER. It may take a while with his wife."

When Joe came home at 4:00 a.m., he related a horrific event. Lydia Baker had rampaged through their kitchen, smashing everything in reach with a hammer. Baker wrestled it from her, but in the process they both fell. She broke a hip. He sprained an ankle.

Rona and her mother arrived a day later. Nora Baker, a thin blonde who looked older than her years, told Amy the doctors had persuaded her father to put Lydia into a memory care facility.

"She aimed for the control panel of every appliance," Nora said. "Like she was gunning for anything she couldn't understand any more. Their kitchen is ruined."

Compassion overcame past history; and Amy insisted the Bakers come for dinner, including Mookie.

When she told the kids, Josie cried, "No-o-o! I'm going to bed right now."

"I'll eat if I can wear what I want to," Connor said.

"You always do," Amy sighed.

With a throbbing head she began dinner, and second thoughts set in. Why had she issued the invitation? She squeezed in seven places at the breakfast table and suppressed an irrational urge to blame Baker for the damaged dining room table. When the doorbell rang, she kicked her too-tight shoes off her feet and answered the door barefooted.

Dazed and pathetic, Baker arrived on crutches with an open-toed nylon boot on one foot and a sandal on the other. Nora settled him into a kitchen chair. Rona and Mookie followed, looking for Josie but finding only Gypsy, who greeted them with the forgiving amnesia of dogs.

Conversation lurched from weather to gardening to pets—each topic abandoned when it approached a sore spot, like lightning, sprinkler heads, or poop. Amy called the children to dinner, hoping they could improve the conversation.

Connor arrived in a suit of armor.

"How're you gonna eat in that thing?" Rona pointed at his plastic helmet.

He flipped up the visor. "Like this," he squeaked in his silliest voice.

Josie appeared in a pink nightgown and fluffy bedroom slippers. Ignoring Rona, she squeezed in between Connor and Amy.

Connor's visor clacked open and shut with each bite. Josie spoke only in whispers, and Rona exaggerated every word, trying for a reaction from Josie. The adults uttered banalities as they passed biscuits and butter. The dogs settled hopefully under the table.

At last Nora broached the dreaded subject, which seemed less painful than current conversation.

"So we found a facility nearby for Mom," she said. As she elaborated on schedules and programs, they realized David Baker had put his forehead down beside his plate. His shoulders shook.

"I'm going to miss her so," he sobbed.

Nora put an arm around him and patted his thinning hair. Amy wiped her eyes with her napkin. They returned to eating, silently, awkwardly, until Josie squealed.

"There's a hairy bug on Gypsy!"

Joe ducked under the table.

"Ouch! That was my foot," cried Amy. "Did you get it?"

"It's nothing but a piece of wood mulch," he reported and returned to his seat. Silence descended again.

"Hey, who's rubbing my feet?" Josie demanded, glaring at Rona.

"Not me," Rona said. "I'm rubbing Mookie's tummy."

From the depths of the knight's helmet Connor said, "The dogs are both here by me, stupid."

"But I thought . . ." said Rona.

"That's my slippers," said Josie.

A moment later Baker raised his head with a start. "Who's licking my toes?"

"It's Gypsy," cried Rona.

Baker lifted Gypsy to his lap. She squirmed to reach his face and began licking his salty, tear-streaked cheeks. He began to smile. "I had forgotten how good it feels to be kissed by a dog." He hugged Gypsy to his shoulder like a baby, stroking her fur.

"We always used to have dogs, Dad," said Nora. "You should get another one."

"I can recommend a good invisible fence company," Joe offered.

"I could train him with my wand," Connor said through his visor.

"Uh-oh. Mookie's chewing at my boot." Baker set Gypsy down to shoo Mookie away.

Three kids dived under the table, giggling and whispering. Then Rona said, "Now!"

"What . . .?" Joe exclaimed as his loafers sailed into a corner.

"My shoes!" Nora yelped. "What are you putting on my feet?"

"M-m-m, a creamy foot massage." Amy smiled. "Wait! Where did the butter dish go?"

"I'm getting a foot bath from a dog!" Joe exclaimed.

Baker began to laugh. "This is the happiest dinner I've had in years."

"Was that sarcasm?" Josie whispered.

"I don't think so," replied Connor, tossing his helmet into a corner.

Under the round table, three children giggled.

Solitude

by
Sharon Rice

Summer with you in a cottage
by the sea,
plain-walled and carpeted
with strewn sand.

Long hours of separate solitude,
mind as clean as a monk's cell
and pores wide open
to the salt and you.

Nightfall.

In it come rest
and companionable solace
as of the first garden.

Picker Singin' on the Step

by
Marilyn Lorenz

Summer is a-comin' cross the cornfield,
Down the river,
Summer is a-comin' in
Chuck Will's Widow's call,
Summer is a-comin' down my back
And in my eye,
Summer is a-comin' cross the sky.

I been a-watchin' fer it, lo these many
Lonesome days,
I been a-watchin' fer it when I pray.
Summer is a-comin' down the sweat drips
In my brow,
Summer is a-comin'
Soon as now.

And if the Lord'll let me, I'll live through it
One mo time,
And if the Lord'll bless me I'll be strong.
He'll raise me to the pickin'
When the summer growin's in,
and buy my sweetest rest,
when summer's done.

Mountaintop Experiences: Lowcountry Ribs

by
Max D. Judge

R are mountaintop experiences occur at unexpected times in
a lifetime. It has been my privilege to serve as interim
director of the First Presbyterian Day School for one year.
During this short period, Lowcountry ribs provided me with
three peak experiences.

As interim director I was involved in a revision of our
lunch menus and guided the elimination of such carbohydrate-
rich items as spaghetti, noodles, and rice. I worked with Ellie,
the head chef and caterer in the church kitchen, and Sheila,
one of her cooks, whose combined years of cooking
experience I would not try to estimate. Ellie is a mentor for all
who work in the kitchen, and her word is unchallenged
throughout the church on any issue of food service; Sheila has
devoted a lifetime to learning Ellie's recipes. I entered their
environment with some trepidation.

One of my suggested new items was country-style
ribs. Sheila accepted that change with great enthusiasm and
quickly agreed to do a trial run. She prepared the ribs and
served them to the children and teachers to some degree of
acclaim. To my taste, they were just okay.

When I pursued Sheila about her method of
preparation, I realized why my enthusiasm for the ribs was
lukewarm. She had parboiled the ribs the day before and then

reheated them and added the sauce on serving day. Parboiling made ribs tender, she explained. I countered that reheating meat that had not been heated first with vegetables, which provide antioxidants, could produce warmed-over flavor. Sheila rolled her eyes at me and declined to discuss it.

My next step was one that had Jacquie, the administrative assistant at the Day School, and others rolling their eyes at me. My wife called Jacquie and told her to tell Sheila to give up. She made some reference to having lived with me for fifty years, and she knew that Sheila was not going to win. I disregarded all of that. However, I admit that challenging an African-American cook on her method of cooking country ribs could imply that I was intoxicated or extremely naïve at best.

But I had inside information. In my thirty-seven years as a professor of muscle physiology and food science at Purdue University, my graduate students and I spent many years studying oxidative rancidity and conducting research on ways to prevent it in cooked pork. Armed with this knowledge, I charged on with a cooking demonstration. To avoid Ellie's oversight, I conducted my test in the Day School oven, some distance from the church kitchen.

I took one strip of country ribs and put it in a covered dish in the oven at 250 degrees F. Three hours later I uncovered the dish, added the barbecue sauce, and left the ribs in the oven for thirty minutes. Then I called Sheila for a taste test.

She said, "I can tell you right now that it's gonna be tough!"

The meat was extremely tender; and, of course, there was no trace of warmed-over flavor.

Sheila was effusive in her praise. Her final comment was, "I'm gonna tell Ellie about this; you have made a believer out of me!" She now follows my cooking schedule, and the children have grown to love the ribs.

A mountaintop experience in the Lowcountry! What a privilege it is to operate in a diverse, enthusiastic environment and create something of lasting value! Now that the excitement has subsided, I recognize my good fortune in the inexact field of meat cookery; and I now offer a little prayer that I not become so overconfident that I choose future battles that I have no chance of winning. Perhaps this one was close enough.

There was more than one peak to this mountaintop. One is the joy of watching three- and four-year-old children savor those country ribs. The barbecue sauce may dribble down small chins, but that is of little note when lifelong gastronomic memories are being created.

Another peak is the privilege of being counted as one of Sheila's friends. Together we created a product that, in a small way, has extended a simple pleasure to children in their most formative years. I am reminded of that enduring friendship each time I walk into the church kitchen and receive one of Sheila's hearty hugs.

Here is the recipe for Day School Country Ribs as evolved:

Country Style Ribs

<u>Ingredients:</u>

Meat from the Boston butt section of the pork shoulder, cut in 1½ inch strips, with or without ribs in the strips

Barbecue sauce: equal quantities of tart and sweet brands of barbecue sauce diluted with some catsup, a little mustard, and a judicious amount of brown sugar. Mix well. (Amounts are proprietary with Sheila)

<u>Preparation:</u>

1. Place ribs in a covered dish or pan and bake for three hours at about 250F.
2. Remove the cover, remove visible fat and bones, and mix in generous quantities of barbecue sauce.
3. Return to oven with cover removed and allow juice to dehydrate for 30-60 minutes.

Monarch

Photograph by Sansing McPherson

Butterfly Man

by
Raymond P. Berberian

My immigrant father's World War II Bronze Star for Valor spoke volumes about his experiences of death while in the United States Army. It was a topic that we never discussed. However, as he approached his ninety-eighth birthday in relatively good health, I began to suspect he was worried, even afraid, of death. When I noticed then that melancholy increasingly overtook him, I teased that it was an accomplishment to have outlived his enemies *and his friends.* I brought him to stay with my family, hoping this would add to his well-being. However, I increasingly noticed his lapses in memory and bouts of sadness.

One Sunday morning I heard Dad shouting and pounding on the upstairs hall bathroom door. "Open the door! Open the door!" I heard from the lower level of our colonial-style house.

I raced up the staircase, two steps at a time, toward the panicky shouts and sounds emanating from behind the bathroom door. "Hold on Dad! Hold on! I'll get you out," I yelled, only to find the brass door knob locked.

After retrieving a long metal knitting needle, kept handy in the master bedroom for similar calamities involving my children, I poked it into the hole in the door knob. I heard a click. The brass knob turned in my hand, revealing my tee-shirt-clad father with drying shaving cream on his startled face.

"Are you okay?" I asked, noticing the fifty-year-old military razor in his hand.

With a look of despair, Dad indignantly but sincerely asked, "Who locked the door?"

"You must have! It only locks from the inside," I shot back, exasperated at his inability to remember that my interior doors were exactly like those in his old house.

"I was just trying to shave when someone locked me in," he insisted while pawing at the three days of stubble on his face.

Wary of his disorientation and lack of dexterity with the metal razor, I suggested, "Why don't you let me finish shaving you?"

Dad's mood seemed to change. "Okay. Thanks," he said.

As he thrust the silver-colored razor toward my hand, I deftly relieved the soldier of his ancient screw-together device. The ordeal now diminished, I commenced the ritual of stroking his face, washing out the razor, and repeating. It felt odd ministering to him this way. I wondered, *How many times did this old soldier use this two-piece razor during his four years of combat in North Africa and Italy during World War II?*

As I completed the last stroke, shock overtook me when Dad announced to me proudly, as if I were an anonymous barber, "You know, I have a son named Raymond!"

Sadly, it dawned on me. Dad had taken his army field-kit razor from among his collection of war items including military decorations, Bible, and war regalia. He did not recognize that I, his only son, was the person shaving him. His mind was adrift somewhere between 1942 and 1945.

Predictably his bouts with sadness, forgetfulness, and memories of childhood hardship in the old country increased. Finally he needed twenty-four-hour care. Despite Dad's relocation to the well-run nursing home, which he called "the last stop," he thrived there that last year. He made friends and delighted peers with his multiple language skills. My daily visits confirmed that the staff and the residents considered Mr. George a pleasant gentleman. I was pleased that he reacquainted himself with a few people he had known years before.

Often after visits to Dad, my thoughts drifted to earlier times. I remembered my last year of law school in 1968 when I was in love with a New York City girl. I was uncertain about asking my girlfriend to marry me. Needing a little fatherly advice, I waited for a Saturday afternoon and approached Dad in the backyard of our family's residence in Englewood Cliffs, New Jersey.

"Hi, Dad. What are you doing?" I mumbled, oblivious to his toil in digging a long drainage ditch.

Sweaty and close to exhaustion in the August heat, my shirtless dad sought a measure of contrition from his barrister-to-be son when he replied, "Can't you see I'm planting handkerchiefs and umbrellas?"

Self-absorbed but surprised by Dad's sardonic words, I laughed nervously at his stinging little joke. "Want me to give you a hand?" I offered lamely.

"No. No. I can handle it," he answered, satisfied with his extraction of a measure of guilt from me.

"I need to ask you a question, Dad. I'm thinking of getting engaged to Marilyn. What do you think?"

Placing the shovel down slowly on a dirt mound, my father wiped his glistening, soiled brow. I towered above him on the sloping lawn. With brown eyes staring up at his law-student son, the short, well-traveled veteran said tersely, "Free as a butterfly."

"What? What does that mean?" I remarked, confused.

The long-married immigrant then said to me, "Son, when you are single, you are as free as a butterfly!"

His brief words had more meaning than a volume of text books about life, of course; but to his naïve, love-sick son it really had not sunk in. I am sure, though, my father knew on that hot Saturday afternoon that fate would take its course, regardless of his words. My first marriage was not to last.

In early October, 2005, I received a late night call at home. The nursing home's coordinator advised me Dad was found asleep on the floor next to his bed. This situation, along with his runny nose, prompted the night nurse to have Dad taken to a hospital in Emerson, "as a precaution."

Within minutes my wife, Denise, and I arrived at the hospital to check on Dad's condition. "Damn it," I groaned to my wife as we entered the dimly lit, dual-occupancy suite. "They've got a large tube in him and some small tube in his nose." As Denise neared the hospital bed with me, a nurse we had met briefly at the desk joined us. With a gentle but firm shake to my father's shoulder, the nurse said, "Mr. B., your son and daughter-in-law are here. Wake up."

We saw Dad stir, open his eyes, and look around the darkened hospital suite. "Dad, how do you feel?" I asked, relieved that the one-hundred-year-old man had awoken seemingly alert. Elevating himself on an elbow from his reclined position, Dad silently stared at the three blurry human shapes surrounding him. "Dad, the nursing home found you on the floor beside your bed," I said anxiously.

"What?"

"The nursing home sent you here, to the hospital," I explained, raising my voice.

Dad's eyes expressed panic. He repeated, "What?"

Finally, my observant wife pointed to the night stand beyond Dad's bed. Quickly, I lifted Dad's eyeglass/hearing aid device and rushed to fit it on him. I suspected he viewed us as strangers.

Mindful of a few previous embarrassing and humorous misplaced-hearing-aid episodes, my wife softly intoned, "George. George," hoping not to startle Dad once his hearing and sight were securely in place.

"Stop shouting," Father reactively demanded before I could lower the device's volume setting.

"Dad, it's me, Raymond. Can you hear us now?" I uneasily asked him.

"Yes. What am I doing in this place?" he demanded, slowly gathering in the antiseptic-smelling surroundings.

"The nursing home sent you to the hospital. How do you feel?"

Assessing himself, Dad answered, "I don't remember. I feel fine."

"The doctor in attendance had some tests done," Nurse Ballard interjected as she adjusted his pillow. "We'll know a little more tomorrow," she assured, patting him on the hand.

My wife, a former medical technologist, took the nurse aside in the hope of gathering more details. Meanwhile, my eyes could not help but follow the yellowish pink fluid passing through a large tube which was partially obscured by the bed sheets over Dad's waist. Before leaving, I assured him I would return in the morning. Luckily, he was in no pain.

On our short drive home from the hospital, Denise suggested that the admitting physician might have suspected pneumonia. Needless to say, I could not sleep. Instead, I lingered in the family room flipping through decades-old family albums. Sure enough, there were pictures from the 1950s of the old Hackensack, New Jersey, house where I spent my early years. Dad bought the 1901 three-story, wood-framed fortress with brick foundation in the early 1950s. There was a picture of Dad next to his 1954 Pontiac parked on the gravel driveway which ran from the street to the detached garage at the end of our rear yard. The picture brought back a flood of memories.

ᘒᘒᘒᘒᘒᘒᘒᘒᘒ

I recalled that one of my childhood antics had unintentionally injured my father on the driveway. I surely got punished for it—luckily after Dad recovered and simmered down. The occasion involved my testing a bow and arrow set in the rear yard beside the long driveway. I took a large, empty cardboard box and placed it on the loose gravel drive. Reasonably certain no one roamed the vacant lot behind the box, I paced back twenty-five steps to the rear of the house. I then turned to the open box. Its two cardboard flaps faced me. My first two metal-tipped arrows stuck into a box flap. The third arrow hit a flap just as it was caught by a sudden wind gust. The bullet-nosed arrow ricocheted off the flap at a ninety-degree angle down the driveway out of sight. I flinched the moment the deflected arrow went astray.

"Ahh. Ahh," I heard from the unseen side of the house where my father had been washing the Pontiac. I thought the worst but hoped for the best.

With the bow still in hand, I prayed that my father had faked a sound of injury as a lesson to me on safety. Fearfully, I trotted in a leftward arc to reach the rear corner of our house. As I nervously craned my neck around the pussy willow tree at the corner, I saw the red-and-white Pontiac but not my father. Venturing baby steps onto the driveway proper, I noticed my father's sandal-clad feet protruding from a bed of lilies and rose bushes decorating the small space between the driveway and the side of our house.

The sounds were now groans as I approached my father, lying face down in the lilies. *Yup, I got him,* I thought with a wince, *but where?*

Perspiring, I approached closer. The stray arrow had lanced my father in the side of his right foot, through his sock, and exactly between two leather strips of his sandal. He slowly rose from the flower bed. He lifted his bloody foot and yanked the protruding arrow from his flesh. It had penetrated one-half inch above the bottom of his right sole. *An also impossible hit,* I remember thinking.

I stood there silent as a sphinx. Then, my head shrunk into my torso like a turtle. A kid never wants to see his Dad bleed, let alone become the architect of it. Holding the arrow in his right hand, my father looked at his ashen-faced, nine-year-old and quipped with teeth clenched, "Four years I fought in World War II without a scratch only to come home to be shot by my son's arrow!"

Humor in the face of agony, I marveled, moving cautiously away from the simmering man. He limped toward the kitchen door seeking Mom's attention to the odd wound. He glared back at me, probably imagining punishments which would pass muster with Mom. I knew I was off the hook, but only momentarily. Not like the time I threw a Spalding rubber ball through my sister's second-floor bedroom window, and Dad caught me after a block-long chase.

That 1954 photo reminder of Dad and the Pontiac in the driveway of our first home made me chuckle. He looked pretty fit only nine years after the war, but my arrow slowed him down to a limp for a while.

೪•೪•೪•೪•೪•೪•೪

The first few days I visited him at the hospital he looked fine. He said he felt no discomfort except for the lower tube. I assumed he would be released to the nursing home. However, after a week, the physician confided that his organs had been shutting down for quite a while. The pneumonia for which he was admitted only drew attention to the internals of a century-old body.

His physician called a few nights later at about 9:30 p.m. advising that Dad had less than a week to live. The doctor was wrong; he died after midnight. My hundred-year-old dad's passing made me wonder whether in death he had rejoined his sisters and his parents, who never left the old country. He had longed to see them in his melancholy, often crying like a little boy who was lost.

Dad's pain was still fresh on my mind one week after his October death. So I was glad when the weather finally allowed me to cut my overgrown lawn. Solitary yard work had always been an elixir for my troubled soul. As I bent over a rubber trash container shaking grass clippings from the full mower bag, I noticed peripherally a fluttering object contrasted against the white aluminum siding of my house. I ignored the quivering shadow which seemed to disappear from the corner of my eye as suddenly as it appeared. *What could it have been anyway? A bird? A leaf?*

Within seconds the dark, fluttering object reappeared as if indignant at my utter lack of attention. Intrigued, I stood erect and turned to discover a darting Monarch butterfly silhouetted against the expansive siding of the house. Despite the decades I lived in New Jersey, I never encountered a butterfly in late October, let alone a Monarch butterfly. As I bent over to resume my work, my mind flashed that this was Dad's way of signaling me. Instantly elated, I turned to the orange and black apparition. It had vanished. He was "free as a butterfly."

Double Coupons

by
Norm Levy

$1,000,000

ONE MILLION DOLLARS

Off List Price
With This Coupon

May not be combined with any
other offers or price reductions.
One coupon per purchase

The Island Packet Real Estate Section: April 20, 2009
(Coupon in Ad for Palmetto Dunes home listed at
$5,750,000)

A million-buck coupon

Is worth clipping, I'd say.

But, I'll keep careful watch

For <u>double</u> coupon day.

From the Skeleton of Her Story

Frederick W. Bassett

She haunts me with his black and white cows in tow.
For twenty years she had endured them, their udders
bursting twice a day as they wait for that cupped
suction to pull them dry. From the kitchen window,

she watched him head for the barn once again, black
rubber boots squishing through rain-sodden stench.
Always that tangle of Holsteins pulling her down.
She recalled her one year of college. Those dreams

exchanged for a fleet-footed halfback when death
called him home to run the family dairy.
She needed a second chance. Would he understand?
Two courses, two mornings a week for one semester.

Not a generous concession. But she grabbed it
and commuted sixty miles to the college of her youth.
In room 205 of Davis Hall, she sat against the wall
on the second row without question or comment.

I knew her name, the hunger of her eyes,
and I counted on her attention to power my lectures.
The last day, she stopped by the office, restrained
at first, then a swollen stream rushing for the sea.

Needing more, I shared green tea and praised
her keen intellect, the passion of her essays.
Bone by bone, I unearthed the skeleton
of her story and then watched her back disappear.

White Egret
by
Bob Hamel

I came to the pond that summer day
Delighted to see her on the grassy knoll,
Curved neck of pristine snow,
Smooth yellow bill,
And long, railed black feet.

Startled, she jumped, the heavy air
Flowing into responding lungs,
Over soft layered white plumes,
Long, sleek, angel wings
Skimming over the beckoning pond.

"Where are you going?"
I asked.
Suddenly, a calculated dive,
A watery explosion,
A fish snatched from hiding reeds.

She swallowed the little fellow whole.
I watched its passage
Down her long, eager neck.
Ah, your dinner today.

Be at peace, my snowy friend.
This is what you do.
A death, a meal,
A survival.

You are protected now
To path the barren sky.
My heart skips a beat
Anticipating your portrait
For yet another day.

Ali Gator

Acrylic by Jane Anderson

A Gator Can Hope

by
Will Anderson

Pickings in the lagoon and environs had been poor for ages. The cat that Ali Gator recently caught, drowned, and swallowed whole was completely digested. Hunger pangs had begun to monopolize his thoughts. But all that changed when George and Lacy Johnstone arrived for a stay in one of the rental homes that bordered the lagoon—and culminated days later in a wee hour when Lacy, fresh from bed, dressed only in a thin negligee, her feet bare, cracked open a hall door and peeked into the dark kitchen.

Ali, huge, prehistoric, wet, and glistening in the sudden light coming from the hall behind Lacy, stopped in mid snap at the piece of prime sirloin steak lying on the kitchen floor. And with jaws still open, lifted his head and stared curiously.

Lacy screamed!

Ali thought, *Stop screaming. I'm not that ugly.*

ଚ୍ଚ-ଚ୍ଚ-ଚ୍ଚ-ଚ୍ଚ-ଚ୍ଚ

Days earlier, in an older BMW heading south on Interstate 95, George Johnstone drove with hands tight on the wheel, listening as his wife, Lacy, read out loud from a travel book that told of Hilton Head Island. She was doing her best to cheer him, but nothing helped. His up-scale men's clothing store in New Jersey had gone under thanks to the feeble economy. He spent every cent he had trying to save it, but to no avail. He was now dependent on his wife—money from a large trust she had inherited. The trip was her idea. He had agreed, reluctantly.

"Would you please stop reading that book out loud," he snapped.

"Aren't you the pleasant one," she snapped back, shutting the book. "No need to take your hostility out on me. It's not my fault the store failed."

He was quiet for a long moment, but anger got the better of him. "If you'd given me that loan, it would not have failed."

"Good money after bad, George. Another month and it would have failed anyway. And my money would be down the drain."

George opened his mouth to argue the point but stopped. He couldn't win. It was her money, her decision.

"Let's forget the store and have a good time," she pleaded. "We're going to Hilton Head. Sun, fun, beach, golf . . ."

George lied. "Sure, hon. We'll forget the store and have a good time."

She smiled, opened the book, and began reading out loud again. His grip on the wheel tightened even more.

They had married a year earlier. George was handsome, dressed well spent lavishly, and had a charming way with women. She was pretty and fun to be with, but her money was what attracted him—the marriage an investment. The economy was failing and his business along with it. He never dreamed she would not help save it. Now he was stuck in a relationship he no longer wanted with no easy way out.

Two hours and pages and pages later, George pulled into the driveway of the house Lacy had rented. Begrudgingly he grabbed their bags, followed her inside, and listened as she extolled its many features. All he could think of was the rental fee and how many days it would have kept his store afloat.

After touring the house they went out back, through a kitchen door, onto a patio that overlooked a lagoon. Scrappy the Squirrel, startled on seeing them, dropped the acorn he was working on and dashed up a tree and out of sight.

"How cute," Lacy mused. Scrappy smiled.

"A rat with a fluffy tail," George muttered. Scrappy glowered.

While she chatted on about the landscaping and flowers, he walked to the water's edge. When he first saw it, it looked like a log. But logs don't have eyes. And logs don't propel themselves through the water. He stepped back.

When Lacy saw it, her mouth dropped, her eyebrows rose, and her eyes widened. "That's an awfully large alligator," she said. "We'll have to be careful out here. They can be very dangerous."

George laughed. "Silly woman," he said with contempt. "Just don't try to pet it, and you'll be okay." He started to say, *Don't feed it and you'll be okay*, but the germ of an idea changed his mind.

"Be sarcastic if you like," she said. "But I read about alligators in that book. An average mature adult weighs 800 pounds, is thirteen feet long, and can run as fast as we can for a short burst. This one looks even bigger than that. And if they get a grip on you with those jaws and those seventy-five teeth," she added, "you'll never get loose."

He gave Lacy a long stare. The idea was diabolical . . . but perfect. The house was built on a concrete slab, the patio at the same level. The lawn sloped smoothly from the patio down to the lagoon.

He started the second night. They had spent the day at the beach—Lacy swimming, walking, and picking up shells; he sitting in a chair under an umbrella, staring out at the water mulling over the idea. She was tired and went to bed early. When she was asleep, he took a steak from the freezer, cut off a piece, walked down to the lagoon, and dropped it near the edge.

Just an experiment, he rationalized. Minutes later from the patio he saw the alligator eye the meat, slide out of the water, and grab it with one snap of its jaws.

The next day, without Lacy's knowledge, George bought several steaks. He put them in a cooler, added ice, and hid the cooler in a kitchen closet. That night and for several more successive nights he got out of bed when Lacy was asleep and put out a piece of steak—closer to the house each night—and watched the alligator devour it. Then he dumped the water from the cooler, added new ice, re-hid the cooler, and crawled back into bed. Lacy was a sound sleeper, particularly after an active day.

On the last day George pretended to sprain his back. That night, with only one steak remaining, he dropped it a few feet inside the kitchen. He left the outside door open and turned the lights off. When he saw the alligator climb out of the water, he quickly got back into bed.

"Lacy!" he said loudly and waited until her eyes opened. "I heard something in the kitchen. Maybe it's that damn squirrel. I don't think the back door closed all the way. Can you take a look? I can't move . . . my back is killing me."

Lacy lay still for a moment waiting for her mind to waken fully and her eyes to focus. George had become more pleasant as the days passed. She sensed he was faking the back ache, but no matter. His mood was better, and the days more enjoyable. She got out of bed.

Ali had been floating a few feet from shore. Only his eyes were above the water when he saw the man wave the piece of steak and drop it a few feet inside the kitchen. Ali flicked his tail, glided to shore, and began his awkward climb up the lawn to the house. When he reached the kitchen door, he crossed the threshold and waddled toward the steak. That was when the room filled with light, and he saw the woman and heard her scream.

Ali's eyes quickly focused back on the steak—he had grown to love its taste. He would eat and run.

The woman's scream grew louder, however, and Ali looked up again. She had tried to back out of the kitchen into the hall, but the man had come up behind her, given her a violent shove, and propelled her into the room. *A month of steaks*, Ali thought.

But the woman turned as she fell, grabbing the man's arm. Her momentum carried them both down. They landed next to Ali. *Two months of steaks.*

"Take him, not her," Scrappy the Squirrel yelled from his tree just outside the kitchen. "She said I was cute. He said I was a rat with a fluffy tail."

Ali agreed, not because of Scrappy's comment, but because the man had slipped on the piece of steak and his legs were inches from Ali's powerful jaws.

Snap!

Lacy, her eyes fixed on George, slid across the kitchen floor toward the hall as the alligator pushed himself through the open back door. George went with him, but not by choice. The alligator's jaws were clamped across his lower legs. George grabbed at the doorframe as he was pulled through, but he could not hold on.

Lacy reached the wall next to the hall door, rested her back against it, and stared at the piece of steak. Realization hit like a ton of bricks: the unhappy marriage, the trust that George would inherit on her death, the fake pleasantness, his directive to go to the kitchen, and his severe shove toward the alligator. Days earlier, she had noticed the cooler partly filled with steaks. George told her the freezer was full. It was not, but she had not wanted to argue.

He had lured the alligator with the steaks. She should be heading down to the lagoon!

She put her hands to her ears to block the screams. She shut her eyes, grimaced, and did not move.

She never saw George again. No one did.

Ali was not hungry for weeks thanks to George. Then another couple rented the house.

A *gator can hope,* he told himself while cruising by the house on their first night.

Old Ford

by
Art Cornell

I remember in the back seat
Of an old Ford
A friend had in the 50s—
Learning love—yeah—
Arms and legs akimbo
And enthusiasm
And fear and ignorance
And God knows what—
And it was not pretty,
And it was not love.
And when I got married
In '62
On my wedding day
My dad asked me,
"Is there anything you want
To know?"
Like he had answers,
Or I had questions . . .
And it took me the better part
Of a lifetime
To learn love,
The kind that gets under
Your skin—
The kind that gets under
Your fingernails
When you scratch at life.

Good Dog

by
Bobbi Hahn

Soon after my husband and I moved with our three young sons to a small Ohio town, one of God's most precious creatures found her way to us.

She was beautifully trained. Since her coat and pads showed no signs of wear or hard living, I assumed she had just recently gotten away from her owner. I advertised in every local paper and checked with all the vets in the area. Surely someone was grieving her loss! I leashed her and took her for long walks, hoping she would find her way home. The only thing she found was the scent of a few rabbits that had earlier crossed our path.

When it became clear that we were not going to find her owner, my boys began the delicate process of choosing her name. After much deliberation it was selected: "Pooch." I thought such a sleek, elegant canine deserved a name more indicative of her appearance and temperament, but I was resoundingly outvoted.

She was a shiny, black Labrador retriever, perfect in every way except for the absence of a tail. Since she was a stray, our vet had no way of knowing if she had been born that way, lost it in an accident, or had it surgically removed.

When she found us, she was young, although not quite a puppy. As my boys grew, she matured along with them. She played ball, kept them warm, and tolerated the gradual addition of three cats to the household.

She never understood that she was a seventy-five-pound dog. When a cat sat on the deep windowsills of our big, old Victorian house or dozed on the arm of the sofa, Pooch attempted to do likewise with predictable and hilarious results. I tried not to let her see me laugh, for she had great dignity and would have been humiliated. She thought she was a lap dog and would curl herself up into the smallest possible configuration as I sat reading, my legs falling quickly asleep from her weight.

She also saved our lives. One day while my husband was at work, the boys and I went upstairs to take naps. Pooch usually joined us, sharing herself equally among my bed and those of the boys. But on this day she would not settle down and persisted in jumping on the bed, head-butting me, and pushing her cold nose forcefully into my hand. When I did not get up, she began barking. Not wanting her to awaken the boys, I followed her downstairs, as she seemed to want me to do. In the kitchen I found that the pilot light on our ancient stove had gone out, slowly filling the house with deadly gas.

Years passed, and our sons graduated from high school, went on to college, and moved on with their lives. Pooch remained with me, my faithful companion and steadfast provider of vast quantities of unconditional love.

Gradually she began having difficulty walking, and her eyesight began to fade. Over time, the vet and I had frequent talks. We constantly re-evaluated her condition because we wanted her to live as long as possible yet not to suffer or be in pain. Eventually, when she was fifteen, the time came for the vet and me to have the talk that no pet owner ever wants to experience, about a decision no pet lover ever wants to make.

I brought each of the cats to her to say their goodbyes. Then I curled up next to her, thanking her for the joy she had brought to us, for being a hero and saving our lives. I told her how very much we loved her. Between sobs, I said, "I really don't want to do this." I wrapped her in her favorite blanket and got into the back seat of a friend's car for our last ride together. Talking to her all the way, I petted her beautiful, regal lab head and hugged her tightly against me. I know the exact moment that her spirit left her body with a sigh.

I carried her into the vet's office and said, "She's already gone."

The vet put a stethoscope to her chest and confirmed what I already knew, adding, "She knew you didn't want to have to do this, so she made it easy for you. She always was a good dog."

No-See-Ums

by
Greg Smorol

In the cool of night
Or the heat of day,
There is no problem
At work or play.

It's the time between
When they move forth,
The scourge of the South,
Not found up North.

They are so tiny,
They can hardly be seen,
They're so pesky,
You know they're mean.

They spoil your fun
And make you mad,
Your day seems ruined,
And you feel sad.

The good news is
They come with the season,
And the rest of the year
Is nice beyond reason.

There are two weeks here
And two weeks there
That are the burden
That we must bear.

In the South as we know,
It's sunny most every day,
That's not free though,
'Cause no-see-ums make us pay.

But if that price,
Seems high to you,
Then move up North,
To the cold and flu.

<——1/8"——>

No See Um, aka "biting
midge," Genus: *Culicoides.*

Earth Day, Every Day

by
Bob Hamel

Oh, dragonfly, oh, dragonfly
what a delight you are,
transparent wings,
green elongated body,
fragile as a needle.

How majestic against the
forming clouds and
present blue of the sky,
forcing the wind.
You swoop, you turn, you climb.

The wren said to the chickadee,
"Did you see that he can
hover like a helicopter?"
What dexterity!
They made way for him
wondering where he was going.

At last we see it's the crafty
ambiguous mosquito
that you seek,
filling your appetite
by the dozens.

Nature is so perfectly balanced
we learn so much each day.
Our role is to be stewards
of the earth.
Why do we abuse it so?

The Legend of Clipper Gates

by
Len Camarda

Dom Liguori was a horror on the golf course. He was very serious about the game—too serious—and became irritable if things did not go his way. He was not a club thrower—yet—but he could become obscenely profane if he sliced a ball into the trees, plunked one in the water, or missed a putt. His verbal tirades had been characterized as capable of peeling paint. Birds stopped singing; squirrels stopped to stare, wide-eyed and petrified; and gators quickly submerged if they were in the vicinity of his abusive rants. *Maybe he'll play well today and we'll be spared*, was the hope of the morning for his assigned playing partners.

Dom was a retired finance executive who, off the golf course, was regarded as a pleasant guy. On the golf course, however, he became his evil twin, a Jekyll and Hyde transformation that seemed to be getting worse. He played golf three times a week and generally shot in the low nineties. That gave him a handicap of nineteen, about average for the group he played with at Port Royal Golf Club on Hilton Head Island; but he felt driven to lower his handicap. He practiced by himself almost every afternoon on the Robbers Row course, where he and his wife had a home off the tenth fairway. Dom walked the course those afternoons, practicing everything, but more and more focusing on his putting, the weakest part of his game.

❧❧❧❧❧❧❧❧

On an overcast Tuesday afternoon, almost five o'clock, there were some flashes of light and distant thunder out to the east. *A storm might be brewing*, thought Dom, but it looked far away. He was on the thirteenth hole, trying his tenth putt from the back of the green to the cup located in the left front corner of the green. Again his downhill putt tailed off to the left and off the green, frustrating Dom.

"You have to aim your ball two cups to the right and think about hitting it to a spot halfway to the hole. Then it will fall in," a voice said from the little hill overlooking the green near the cart path.

"Where the hell did you come from?" a surprised Dom answered.

"Around here," the man responded, walking down the hill. "Look," he beckoned to Dom, crouching down and pointing to the putting surface. "There's a little swell about halfway to the hole. You just have to get to there and then let the slope carry your ball to the hole. Not many players recognize that little swell, which is why most putts miss to the left and roll off the green. Stroke it easy."

Dom dropped a ball to the green, aimed his putt two cups—about ten inches—to the right, and stroked the ball. It looked as though the ball was going to stop about halfway to the hole. Dom pursed his lips and looked at the man, thinking, *Why am I listening to you?* Then the ball ever so slowly began to pick up speed, moving toward the cup. It gently rolled to the left and then, *plunk*, dead center in the hole.

"Hey, that was great," exclaimed Dom, walking towards the man. "What's your name? I'm Dom Liguori." He extended his hand.

"Clipper, Clipper Gates," the man said, turning away and looking back at the balls that had rolled off the green.

Dom drew his hand back, shrugging at the bad manners of the young man. "You said you're from around here. Port Royal Plantation, I assume?"

"Oh, yes," the young man replied, "been here a long time."

"Then how is it I don't . . .?" Dom never completed his sentence as a flash of lighting and boom of thunder shook the ground. "*Jeez, where the hell did that come from?*" he said, looking behind him. Turning back, he was all alone. Clipper Gates was nowhere in sight.

Must of scared the crap out of him. Dom chuckled to himself and started to walk briskly back home, hoping to beat the rain. *It's amazing,* he thought. *Never saw this guy in my life, and he knows the green like he's the club pro. Better. I gotta check him out in the club directory.* "Clipper Gates," he said.

The thunder and lightning that scared Clipper Gates off never produced a drop of rain. *Weird,* Dom thought. While Lena, his wife, busied herself preparing dinner, Dom went upstairs and pulled out his Port Royal directory. *Gates, Clipper Gates,* he murmured as he flipped through the pages. *No Gateses,* he said to himself. *Weird.*

ও-ও-ও-ও-ও-ও-ও-ও

The next afternoon Dom went out for his solitary practice round. As usual, he started out on the par-four tenth hole and was playing pretty well. By the time he teed off on the thirteenth hole, the sky became overcast.

What-the-hell? he thought. *It was supposed to be clear all day. Damn, I wanted to get in a full eighteen holes before dark.*

Dom's tee shot was good, just missing the large sand trap on the right of the fairway. He put his approach shot just short of the green. Today the hole location was in the middle of the green, but to the right. Dom's ball was about thirty feet away. He decided to use a seven iron and run the ball up close.

"Good choice of club," Dom heard as Clipper Gates came walking down the cart path next to the hill to the right of the green. "How are you going to play it?"

"Thought I'd run it up about a foot-and-a-half to the left of the hole and hope the ball slides up close," Dom said as he lined up the shot.

"Too much," Clipper said, now behind Dom looking toward the hole. "Looks like it breaks a lot more than it does. Not more than eight inches."

Dom looked at Clipper, smiled, moved over the ball, and gently hit it. The ball flew about one inch off the ground for about three feet, bounced softly, and then began to roll up the slope toward the hole. About five feet from the cup the ball began to move to the right, and sure enough, *plunk*, slid in the hole from the left side of the cup.

"I'll be damned, a birdie," exclaimed Dom. "I never had a birdie on this hole, never."

"Well, you had two good shots to get real close," observed Clipper. "The rest, no big deal."

"Whoa, this *is* a big deal," said Dom. "You gotta be quite a golfer or a great caddie. Which is it?"

"Neither. I just know these grounds real well, and I can read the greens like the back of my hand. It's a useless talent, really," replied Clipper, starting to walk back the way he came a few minutes ago.

"Hey, where you goin'?" Dom shouted. "In a hurry?"

Clipper laughed. "No, ain't got no hurry. No hurry at all. Just promenading."

"Well how about *promenading* with me for a few holes? Are you as good with the other greens as you are on this one?"

"Maybe. Sure, we can do that." Clipper Gates waited at the top of the hill for Dom to catch up with him.

"So where do you live?" asked Dom as they walked along Oak Creek Drive on the way to the fourteenth tee box.

"Fort Walker," he replied.

"Oh, I live nearby, in the Robbers Row section off of the tenth fairway," Dom said. Then, for the first time, he began to study this guy who seemed to appear out of nowhere. He was young, maybe late twenties, early thirties. Dirty blond hair worn long, covering his ears but well short of the shoulders. He had on a gray-and-white striped, long-sleeved pullover made out of what appeared to be coarse cotton, and his trousers were blue jeans, a very light blue.

They reached the fourteenth tee, a 444-yard par five that overlooked Fish Haul Creek. Dom pulled out his driver, went through his pre-shot routine, and then hooked a drive over a row of live oaks and onto Outpost Lane. The ball hit the roadway and bounced out of bounds and out of sight.

"God damn it," shouted Dom, slamming his driver to the ground. "Where the hell did that come from? Son-of-a . . ." and he took another ball from his bag. Again, he went through his practice ritual and promptly sent another ball down Outpost Lane, trying its darndest to catch up with its predecessor.

Dom then recited a litany of expletives. There was deadly silence. The birds stopped chirping. Even the crows stopped cawing. The squirrels turned and bolted away, perhaps in search of a friendlier plantation. Dom finally ended his tirade and rammed his driver into his golf bag.

Clipper stood in silence, his hands in his pockets, staring at Dom. Just then a low rumble of thunder reached a crescendo with an enormous explosion, and lightning lit up the sky.

"Jesus," exclaimed Dom, turning to look toward the light-and-sound show behind the fairway. Dark clouds appeared but just as quickly began to move off toward the ocean. The sky even started to brighten.

Turning back to Clipper, Dom was dumbstruck. Nobody there!

"What the hell . . .?" Dom said out loud. "Where'd he go?" He shook his head and thought, *What a weird guy*, then got his things together and went on to the next hole on his own.

෴෴෴෴෴

The next day Dom played with his group on the Barony course. He had a decent day, shooting ninety; but again his downfall was putting. Barony had easier greens than Robbers Row; but for whatever reason, he had at least a half dozen putts go exactly where he wanted, but the ball just did not make the break he expected.

That's six stokes I could have chopped off my score, fumed Dom, as his companions quickly said their goodbyes.

That afternoon Dom decided he would concentrate only on pitching and putting in his solitary practice round. When he reached the fourteenth tee box, he thought of those two horrendous shots from yesterday, probably still bouncing down Outpost Lane. *Ugh,* he thought with a shudder and continued to walk towards the green. He stopped about fifty yards short of the green, where he could easily be after two good shots. As he was taking a few practice swings, out of the corner of his eye he saw movement near the tree adjacent to the green. He stopped, looked up, and saw Clipper Gates leaning against the tree. He was dressed in the same pullover and jeans he had on yesterday.

"Good afternoon," yelled Dom.

"Likewise," said Clipper. "You'd be best with a high lofting club, like a sand wedge. Try to land in the middle of the green, about five feet from the left edge. From there the ball should nestle close to the hole."

Dom tried four balls with the sand wedge and then walked up to the green to see the results. Two of his balls were within four feet of the hole, and two others were about ten feet away. Clipper then guided him on each of the putts, and he made all four. The ten-footers especially pleased him.

"Can you accompany me for a few more holes? I promise to keep the lightning and thunder away."

"Sure," said Clipper, "but don't make promises you can't keep."

"Oh, today I can. Look at that sky. Not a cloud."

"Well, if you say so," replied Clipper, as the light in the sky suddenly dimmed, and the afternoon became overcast. Way off in the distance, flashes of light danced in the sky.

"Come on, you want to play golf," Clipper yelled, taking the lead and walking toward the tee box for the par three, fifteenth hole.

Dom looked at Clipper and then to the sky. "What the . . . ?" he murmured and then took off after his strange new golf instructor.

❧❧❧❧❧❧❧❧

To reach the fifteenth tee box from the fourteenth green, they followed the cart path, which passed between a couple of houses and then crossed Outpost Lane. Dom noticed a car coming down the road at about twenty-five miles per hour. Dom was about fifty feet behind Clipper when he saw him walk into the street, directly in front of the oncoming auto.

"Stop, Clipper, stop," Dom yelled, dropping his bag and running toward the street.

It would be too late. Clipper was in the middle of the road when the car reached him and continued moving, as if he were not there.

"No, no!" Dom screamed; and the car, a late model Cadillac, screeched to a halt about thirty feet past where Dom was standing. An elderly man got out. He was clearly shaken. "What happened?" he asked. "What happened?"

Dom looked up and saw Clipper standing on the other side of the road, looking at him and the scared driver. "Are . . . are you all right?" Dom stuttered, looking at Clipper.

"Of course I'm all right," Clipper and the driver of the Cadillac answered simultaneously.

"Are you out of your mind?" the driver yelled at Dom. "What the hell is the matter with you?"

"I'm sorry," stammered Dom, looking at the old man and then at Clipper, and back to the old man again. "I thought I saw, uh, uh, a dog. A dog. I thought I saw a dog run in front of your car. I guess you missed it. Thank God. I'm sorry." The old man got back in his car mumbling something that Dom did not understand. The car moved away; and Dom walked to the street, looking at the ground where Clipper Gates should be lying. But there he was, on the other side of the street, perfectly safe and unharmed. *It couldn't be.*

"How did you do that? There is no way he could have missed you. What's going on?" Dom asked, now backing away from Clipper.

"Nothing. He missed me. That's all," replied Clipper, walking towards Dom.

"No. Don't. I can't do this," Dom said. "I don't feel so well. I've gotta go." And he turned, picked up his bag, and began jogging back past the fourteenth fairway all the way back to his house.

෴෴෴෴෴෴

Dom could not get the incident out of his mind.

That car went right through him. He should be dead, but that car went through him. Then he began to think about how the weather changed when Clipper came around and how he would disappear during the thunder and lightning incidents.

Dom stopped going out for his late afternoon solitary practice rounds. He even cancelled his morning games with his playing group. Lena was sure he was coming down with something.

Then one afternoon Dom was sitting in his Carolina room. It was around the time when he typically would be leaving for a practice session. Looking out towards the tenth fairway, he saw Clipper looking back at him. Still in his striped pullover and light blue jeans, he stood there, hands in his pockets.

A chill went through Dom. He sat there for several long minutes. Neither he nor Clipper moved. Then Dom took a deep breath, got up from his leather armchair, opened the door to the patio, and crossed his back yard, approaching Clipper.

"You don't live here. I checked. Who are you?"

"I'm Clipper Gates, and I never said I lived here."

"Yes, you did. You said you lived in Fort Walker. There is no Gates anywhere in the Fort Walker section of the plantation," Dom said, pointing a shaking finger at the man before him. "And you should be dead."

"One thing at a time. I said I was from Fort Walker. That is absolutely true. I was a Confederate soldier, stationed at Fort Walker in 1861. I was killed when General Sherman and his Union troops attacked us in November of that year. So you see, I am dead."

Dom looked at the young man. Seconds ticked away before he replied. "Yeah, right," and reached out to touch him. His hand went right through the gray and white pullover.

"Holy shit," Dom exclaimed, pulling his hand back and holding it close to his chest, rubbing it with his left hand.

"Don't get too excited; ain't no big deal," Clipper said, holding his hands out in a gesture trying to calm a frightened Dom Liguori.

"Ain't no big deal? Nothing is ever a big deal for you. Are you kidding me? I'm in my back yard talking to a ghost, and it ain't no big deal? Jesus H. Christ!"

"Ah, there you go again. You've been good for a few days, and now you start again. Do we need more thunder and lightning?" Clipper asked.

"No, no thunder and lightning, please," Dom stammered. "And what are you talking about?"

"You obviously don't realize what hallowed ground this is," Clipper replied, turning and sweeping out his right arm. "Forty years ago they started to put houses and golf courses on land that is very special. When the South seceded from the Union in 1861, it was South Carolina that led the secession. Fort Walker was built here, on this ground, at the entrance of Port Royal Sound to guard the coast from Union attack. It wasn't a big fort, mostly dirt and logs; and when General Sherman arrived with thirteen thousand Union troops, we were quickly defeated. Thousands of Confederate and Union soldiers, mostly kids, were killed on this ground; and their spirits still reside here. It's our home."

"And what does that have to do with me?" Dom said in a quivering voice. "Why are you harassing me?"

"Think of how peaceful this land is—or was. The beautiful ocean, marshes and forests full of birds and deer, and all sorts of wonderful critters. Then they chop down the trees, build houses and golf courses. But that's okay; the grounds are kept pretty, flowering bushes added here and there; and we came to know that golf was called a gentleman's game. A quiet and respectful game. And they put landmarks around, telling the people about how special this spot is and the sacrifices that were made here, especially around the Robbers Row course."

"But why me? Why are you here spooking me?" asked Dom.

"This is our resting place, where our spirits linger. You wouldn't go around cursing and yelling in a church or cemetery, would you?"

"No, of course not."

"Then you shouldn't do it here either, out of respect for the young men who lost their lives."

"I'm sorry. I never thought . . . I just never thought . . ."

"I know. That's why we thought you were salvageable. That's why we had a plan. You start behaving like a gentleman, and we'll help your game."

"You said *we*. You're not alone?"

"Like I said, Dom, there are thousands of spirits here, and most of us are good guys. A few good ladies, too. We've had to remind others from time to time about this land and the respect it is due. I think you got the message."

"I did, and you're damn right, uh, I mean *so* right. Thank you, Clipper."

"Thank *you*, Dom. Now how about that practice round? I only got to help you out on a couple of greens. There are fifty-two more out there."

༄༄༄༄༄༄༄

The next year, Dom had his handicap down to twelve. *Twelve!* His playing partners thought he went away for a personality transplant, and now they enjoyed his company. One day, after Dom won first place in the club match play championship, an elderly gentleman approached him, offering congratulations. Fifteen years ago, he had been match play champion three years running.

"I've seen you play, Dom. You are a master on the greens."

"Thanks, thanks a lot; but I got some unique help."

"I guessed it," the man said. "No one knows how to read a green better than Clipper Gates, do they?"

Grandmother

by
Marilyn Lorenz

Up from the couch she arose
With a brown crumb of toast on her nose
In her red gardening pants, she taught me to
        dance
And to walk, and to sit, and to pose.

She let the phone ring in order to sing,
It sat there unanswered and lonely,
And the things that she knew were the
        things the wind blew,
And whispered at night to us only.

If I live to be old and have silver and gold,
The treasure I'll hold closest to me,
Didn't cost me a dime and is older than time,
It's the spirit of her that shines through me.

Learning from Mice

by
Charlie McOuat

NEWS FLASH: We can be young again! A new study shows that Resveratrol, the wonder drug, reverses the aging process in mice and may do the same for humans. It also protects against certain forms of cancer, is an anti-viral, and is a neuroprotector. Therefore it promises to lower the risk of Alzheimer's disease and dementia.

This study showed that mice injected with Resveratrol lived longer and lived better than the control group without the injections. The Resveratrol-enhanced mice kept their hair longer, maintained a youthful appearance, were stronger, and had better stamina on a treadmill. If these benefits could be transferred to humans, we too could live longer and enjoy our lives more along the way.

Resveratrol is one of the chemicals found in some red wines. It is therefore easily accessible, cheap, and does not require a prescription. My wife, Lorrie, and I both want to have longer and healthier lives so we decided to give it a try. One problem is that the dosage injected into the mice was the human equivalent of thirty-two bottles of red wine each day. We decided we had better get started if we were to gain the benefits before our demise.

Lorrie has been a moderate drinker all her life. She seldom, if ever, has more than one glass of wine in the evening. Unlike the pure Lorrie, I am more seasoned. I have nurtured the drinking art begun at college fraternity parties culminating in my present form as a quiet social drinker searching for purpose in retirement.

We both share the common dread of growing older and are willing to try almost anything to remain young. We once drank five gallons of water each from the Fountain of Youth in St. Augustine, Florida. We wound up bloated, and we flooded all the bathrooms on the drive back to Hilton Head Island. In contrast, this wine study was not superstition, like Ponce de Leon's fountain. This was cold, hard, factual science; and we were hopeful.

On the first day of our new life, we bought fifteen cases of red wine from Sam's Club. That about depleted their supply, but we did not care. We were determined in our pursuit of eternal youth. We showed our seriousness by exercising and watching our food intake throughout the day. At four thirty in the afternoon I uncorked our first bottle of a moderately priced California red wine. Our choice of a Robert Mondavi 2007 Pinot Noir was full bodied with nice legs and pleasing aroma. Lorrie brought out tumblers, much larger than the common red wine glass, signaling that we meant business. By 4:51, when we drained the last of that bottle, I noticed her wrinkles had disappeared and her cheeks took on a red, youthful appearance.

We sat on the couch and snuggled. I took her hand and said, "Lorrie I had forgotten how blue your eyes are. And your hair glows like when we were dating."

She smiled, turned her head coyly to the side and winked at me. "Oh Charlie, I think you're feeling the wine." She swiped her lips with high gloss lipstick and laid her hand on top of mine. Her red lips and blue eyes accentuated her blond hair and alabaster skin. "That shirt brings out the deep color in your eyes, Charlie. You have that youthful sparkle, but we can't delay our mission. Shall we attack that second bottle?"

At 4:59, I uncorked a bottle of 2006 California Merlot. Neither of us gave a damn about its bouquet or legs. We threw our cherished tumblers into the fireplace, giggled as they crashed against our white birch logs from Maine, and gulped the Merlot from pint beer mugs. We had to drink fast if we were to gain the full health benefits. I sang "Love Song" from *Romeo and Juliet*, in Italian, which I had never spoken before. She glided over our bare kitchen floor like a teenager as she danced her first ballet.

"Jeesh, honey, I didn't know you were sush a good dansher," I exclaimed.

"I din't either," she slurred. "And hey, Charlie, you're looking younger every minute." She was sexy even when she stumbled.

I was now singing, "All I Ask of You" from *Phantom of the Opera*. She joined me, as Christine, my romantic partner. Neither of us had realized we were so talented. Her eyes were beginning to glaze over, but we knew we had to persist if we were going to get young again.

At 5:21 I wrestled, twisted, and somehow uncorked our third bottle. It was some kind of red stuff. Although the outside temperature was thirty-nine degrees, we opened all the windows. We wanted to share our newfound talent with the neighbors.

"Hey, honey, you shing like you did twenty yearsh ago when you were a sholoish in church."

"You're right there, Chuckie boy. I am better now. Aged to perfecshon jush like thish red wine."

The details now get a bit fuzzy, but we woke up at 8:39 p.m., sprawled out on the living room couch, hugging and assuring each other that we indeed seemed younger. We managed to stagger into bed, stumbling over the empty third wine bottle along the way. Being young and healthy can take a lot out of a person. The next day and the day after that we slept, medicated our headaches with aspirin, and reexamined our quest for youth.

Santee-Cooper Swamp

Photograph by Jane Hill

An Unspoken Promise

by
Greg Smorol

Frank was checking out the brand-spanking-new boat attached to Billy Joe's old truck in the parking lot when Billy Joe came up behind him and said, "What d'ya think of my new boat?"

Frank's head snapped around as he came face-to-face with a smiling Billy Joe. "Wow, it's a real beauty. How could you afford to buy this rig?"

Billy Joe grinned. "I didn't buy it. I won it in the Biggest Gator Contest. Ya got to hear the story about how me and Jimmy got the gator; it's a doozie."

Knowing Billy Joe, Frank figured this was going to be a long tale. He had a lot to do, and it would be better told another time over a few beers. "Billy Joe, I just don't have the time right now."

However, Billy Joe was so excited he could not be stopped. Frank quickly interrupted. "Okay, but I'm in a hurry; and you have to finish this story before I count to a hundred. Starting now: One, Two . . ."

Billy Joe began right in on the tale:

The other day me and Jimmy was up in the swampy backwaters of Lake Moultrie looking for a big gator for the contest. We got a little back into the swamp, and we was worried about getting lost—ya know what a maze that swamp is. We was about to turn back when we seen this weird-lookin' guy just a-standin' on a grassy little hill. He had a funny hat bent to form a coupla points and a long-collared coat that seemed sorta odd for a swamp man.

He said, "Hello, boys. I see y'all are looking for a big gator. I know where there's a huge ol' critter jist up a piece. Biggest one I ever seen. Come on; I'll lead y'all to him."

Well, we was sorta wary; but we wanted ourselves a big'un, so we poled our boat along after him. He was a strange ol' guy, but he knew the swamp real good. He'd lead us along and then go amblin' off to the side only to show up again further up. We started to think he was loony because he kept tyin' red ribbons onto the bushes. But the swamp can do that to a fella.

We was a ways into the swamp 'fore we saw a big'un. We was going to get him when the stranger spoke up again. "No, not that one, boys. The big'un is jist a little farther up. Follow me this way."

Well, it was gettin' late, and we needed to head back out soon; but the guy was so persistent that we followed him along. We saw a few more big gators 'fore we came to a large pool deep in the heart of the swamp. The water opened a bit jist in fronta the pool, and there was some sun streamin' down on the opposite bank. When the johnboat was in the opening, that's when we seen him—the biggest gator I ever seen! Me and Jimmy couldn't take our eyes offa him. He looked to be more than eighteen feet, with a head and a row o' teeth like a dinosaur.

We took a dead chicken outta the cooler and stuck it on a big hook tied to our rope. I gave the rope a few twirls and tossed that chicken into the middle of the pond. The gator was a-lookin' at what we done and slid into the water after the chicken. It wasn't but a few minutes when we felt the first tug on the line. We waited for the line to move 'fore we gave it a big yank to set the hook.

Jist then all hell broke loose. That gator rose up right out of the water and came a-splashin' down like a big whale. The rope ran tight, and it took all Jimmy and me could do to hold on.

The fury of the battle lasted for about ten minutes 'fore the gator sunk down and begun a heavy pull away from us. We held on until we figgered the gator done got tired, and we begun pulling it up to the boat. We gained a little ground 'fore the gator got its second wind and took off in a mad frenzy.

We must-a been fightin' for two hours 'fore it seemed the gator was done in. We hauled in the line, hand over hand, until the gator come up beside the johnboat. Jimmy was about to stick his knife in the gator when it attacked us. It flung its huge head sideways and capsized our boat. We was now both in the water with the gator. The rope wound up over the top of the johnboat, so we pulled hard to get the gator's head up and away from us. It was no use. We didn't have no traction in the water, and the gator was goin' down and comin' for us. Jimmy was able to get up on the bank and strung the rope around a tree to help stop the gator *from comin' at me. We held the gator at bay for a while 'fore it decided to come up over the johnboat. It was a smart 'un, all right.*

I would-a been a dead man if it wasn't for the stranger. The stranger was on the bank opposite of Jimmy when he called out, "Here, boys, use this."

He tossed a pistol to Jimmy. When Jimmy caught it, he realized the gun was an ol' flintlock. He drew back the hammer and got as close to the gator as he could and blew its brains out. The ball passed through the gator and our johnboat too. The gator thrashed up. Its head knocked the gun outta Jimmy's hand and into the swamp. We took a moment to catch our breath 'fore we looked up to thank the stranger.

He stood there with a look of fulfillment on his face. He spoke slowly now, sorta reverently. "Thanks, boys. You helped me fulfill a promise I made to myself many years ago. I was hiding in this very spot, with a group of my men when we saw a large contingent of enemy coming our way. We slid down into the water and hid, waiting for them to pass. This same gator came up behind one of my men and clamped down on his leg, pulling him into the pond. The man pulled out his pistol to shoot the gator, but he stopped and looked up at me. He couldn't say anything, or he would give away our position. He tossed me his pistol and his eyes said, 'Come back and kill this gator for me,' as the gator silently pulled him below the surface. I couldn't say anything either, but I vowed to do just that. The pistol I tossed you belonged to the man who gave his life to save ours. I believe this gator embodied an evil spirit, and it took the spirit of that brave man to help us kill it. Thanks again, boys; you've done a good deed."

With that done said, the man started backing into the fog rising up off the swamp water. The fog was growing denser as the cooler air of dusk dropped down to meet the warmer water.

We yelled out, "Wait! How do we get back outta here?"

The stranger was no longer visible, but we heard him say, "Follow the red ribbons, boys; follow the red ribbons."

Jimmy and me got out okay that night, and we turned in the gator the next day. There was a guy there from the Department of Natural Resources who took an interest in the gator right away. It seemed to him, by normal standards, that this ol' gator was over 225 years old. But that couldn't be, 'cause gators only live about fifty to seventy years. He was so interested in that big critter that he packed it up and sent it to his lab to look at it some more.

We never did figure out who that guy in the swamp was, but we got us a strange hunch about him. Jimmy and me. We don't believe in ghosts or that paranormal stuff or nothin', but . . .

"Ninety-nine, a hundred."

Tit for Tat

by
Norm Levy

The Island Packet: May 9, 2009

AMID REVOLT PRICES CUT ON BIGGER BRAS

London—"Britain's largest clothing retailer, Marks & Spenser, has backed down on its incendiary policy of charging a $3 surcharge for bras that are DD or larger in the face of spreading consumer revolt. About 14,000 women gave their name to a Facebook campaign aimed at eliminating the big boob policy."

Bra buyers loudly shouted, "NO"

To prices tagged "pay as you grow."

Consumers raged while proving that

There is power in "tit for tat."

The Blind Leading the Blind:
Two Navigators

by
James Edward Alexander

There had never been a time in my life when I had shared a meal at the same table with a white man. Dining with friends and associates is often a social event, and I was emerging from a system where coloreds and whites, "us and them," were channeled along different social paths by omnipresent COLORED and WHITES ONLY signs. Basic training had changed that, but in that setting each man fed himself. Now I literally held in my hands the awesome power to decide what and in what manner a white man would receive his basic nourishment.

Almost every day in 1951 giant medical air evacuation planes landed at Kelly Air Force base near San Antonio, Texas. They were bringing wounded warriors from the Korean skies and battlefields to the hospital at Lackland Air Force Base, located adjacent to Kelly. One day on Ward 18 we greeted a jet pilot whose face was hidden behind thick bandages. His eyes had been severely damaged in an aerial dogfight, and he was spending his days in darkness. My assignment, as a medical corpsman, was to see and do for him some things he hoped to resume doing for himself someday.

Entering his room, I offered, "Good morning, Lieutenant. Welcome home."

He immediately asked, "What's your name; and are you a doctor, officer, sergeant, or civilian?"

My answer was quick and impolite: "I'm none of the above, sir. I'm a PFC, so I work for a living"

His laughter was so loud that the nurse rushed to his door. It was good to see him in high spirits. When I finally introduced myself as PFC Alexander, James Edward, he asked what name I preferred: Alex, James, Jim, PFC Alexander, or "smart ass."

I told him I preferred James Edward Alexander; and that at least once per day, it would be nice to hear him pronounce it properly.

He responded that he would call me Alex and added, "If you don't like what I call you, just make funny faces at me; since I can't see you, I won't have to ignore you." He laughed some more. Shortly thereafter I delivered the first meal to my special patient, very much sensitive to and appreciating that my distance from Valdosta, Georgia, could be measured in miles; but there was no way to measure the nuances of the social transition taking place.

This person, whose education and training qualified him to pilot a highly technical jet aircraft, was now vulnerable to and relying on the goodness of a stranger. We had traveled along separate passages to the same fork in the road. Fate dictated that we now jointly navigate our new path; but only one traveler, a seventeen-year-old colored boy from Georgia, could see where to steer.

Eating is a very personal function that is influenced by a seemingly endless list of options, including one's selection of seasoning, temperature, shapes, sizes, colors, textures, quantities; whether liquid or solid, raw or cooked, meatless or carnivorous. Other variables to consider are when and where one eats and whether one eats alone.

As I observed the variety of edibles on the patient's tray, I asked, "Do you want me to feed you? Or should I identify your food choices and guide your hand to your plate? Or should I cut your food and fill your fork or spoon so that you can feed yourself?" I simply could not resist adding, "Remember, Lieutenant, if you don't pronounce my name properly, all you'll get will be bread and water."

His answer was acceptable: "James Edward Alexander, you're a disgusting person who was probably run out of your home town."

I interrupted him. "OK, sir, I'll feed you."

Before we proceeded, he said, "Alex, when we're in this room together, please call me Bill." Then he opened his mouth, and I offered Bill the first bite.

A few days later Bill wanted to hear his girlfriend's voice; so he held my arm, and I guided him to the telephone booth at the Red Cross lounge. Two weeks later, just before the noon meal, she came to visit. She offered to feed him, but he declined, jokingly telling her that PFC James Edward Alexander needed the practice. It was an acceptable excuse for her, while masking his real purpose. He and I had refined our dining signals: his rate of chewing; the intervals between helpings, based on texture; the amount of sugar, cream, or lemon he liked in his beverage; and when and how to wipe the crumbs from his face without disturbing his bandages. I was there to feed his body properly, thus giving him the energy to appreciate her presence. She was there to feed his emotions.

Each morning as I entered the ward and greeted the nurses and other corpsmen, Bill would hear my voice and acknowledge my arrival by asking, "Is that you Alex?"

One day he asked me to read to him portions of the *San Antonio Light*, the daily newspaper. In the middle of one article he stopped me and offered this observation and a unique gift: "Alex, I have been observing your manner; and I'll bet that you will one day be a well-educated man. Let me help you get started. It will help me stay alert, and it will help you prepare for college."

His bandages hid from his view the tears that welled in my eyes as I remembered the awful experience during basic training less than three months earlier when, because of my lack of scholarship, I could not complete a simple library assignment. On that day I had knelt in agony and vowed to educate myself. On this day I announced, "Bill, you're repeating the expectations of my grandfather, and you're offering to help me keep a promise to myself. I would appreciate your help."

He then asked me to resume reading but warned that he would stop me when I mispronounced anything and promised to define for me unfamiliar words.

On another day as we visited the Red Cross lounge, we also shopped at the nearby PX, where I purchased a small pocket dictionary. Bill also bought for me a small notebook and a fountain pen. When I arrived for duty the next day, he had memorized a list of subjects that he thought I should know.

He started alphabetically. *Antigone.* I told him to spell his name. He said, "Her name is spelled A-N-T-I-G-O-N-E," then added, "That will naturally lead you to know something about her father *Oedipus,* spelled O-E-D-I-P-U-S, which will introduce you to Greek mythology."

My initial pronunciations of Antigone and Oedipus were "anti-gone" and "o-e-dip-ass." We laughed some more and extended the list to include both history and mythology; the names of famous personalities, living and dead; important dates in history; and a long list of literary classics and music composers.

When we were not learning new things, we were sharing our own histories. In high school he studied chemistry and biology and performed experiments in laboratories. He practiced basketball in a gymnasium and occasionally played in the school's marching band. There was no question that he would go to college, and so he did. Within three months after graduating from college he was enrolled in the Air Force Flight Training Program. He heard that my segregated schools did not have a science lab, gymnasium, or marching band; so I studied chemistry and biology in the same classroom and read about experiments in used books from the white high school. Then, since our family resources were inadequate for me to attend college, twenty-one days after my high school graduation I also entered the Air Force. Our separate roads brought us to this day.

We continued our feeding, reading, and learning rituals. After a couple of months the doctors removed his bandages but shielded his eyes with specially fitted cups that allowed only a trace of light to enter his visual field. Shortly thereafter the doctors informed Bill that he was to be transferred to a VA hospital near his hometown.

Hello is the prelude to goodbye. Between our greeting and the imminent farewell we had exchanged friendship; knowledge; respect; and most profoundly, trust—that sense of mutual faith and confidence. The morning of his departure he wanted to wear his uniform rather than pajamas and robe. We did not talk much as I helped him dress. When he asked, "Alex, how do I look?"

I imitated my basic training flight chief/drill sergeant and said, "I can't hear you." He knew the drill and answered, "James Edward Alexander, you reprobate from Valdosta, Georgia, how do I look?" I gave my approval and walked him to an ambulance for a ride back to Kelly AFB.

We had said hello three months ago; and as we said goodbye, he asked for my hand and said, "Thank you, James Edward Alexander. I hope to see you one of these days."

I replied, "If you do sir, I'll salute you again." And I withdrew my right hand from his, saluted, and added, "Just as I'm doing now."

Today, James Edward Alexander, Esq., lives in Bluffton, SC, and writes stories of a happy military career. This story appears in his book, *Approaching the Forks in the Road.*

Shrimp Boat

Photograph by Bobbi Hahn

Preserving and Protecting Hilton Head Island

by
Norma Van Amberg

Imagine Hilton Head Island, South Carolina, with billboards, bright neon lights, and souvenir shops curbside. Instead visitors praise the natural beauty of this barrier island town, many often describing it as "paradise." Driving on William Hilton Parkway (U.S. 278) they see pampas grass, palm trees, hollies, oleanders, and crape myrtles among the evergreen plantings growing in the grassy medians. They notice how the businesses are set back from the road beyond landscaped buffers.

A five-acre open space with a small wooden sign stating: "This property protected from commercial development by the Town of Hilton Head Island," provides a scenic view of Broad Creek just north of the turn onto the road leading to the Shelter Cove Community Park. It is one of many such signs posted on the island.

Along with the town's planning code—the Land Management Ordinance—a land-banking or acquisitions program established in the early 1990s has helped control development and protect environmentally sensitive lands. It also has preserved property for passive and active parks, wildlife habitat, historic sites, and public beach access.

As of early 2009 the 127 parcels the town had

bought for nearly $150 million totaled about 1,172 acres. This property represents 5.1 percent of developable land within the town limits and 19.24 percent of developable land area outside of the island's planned unit developments (PUDs), according to town records.

Funding comes from the town's quarter-of-a-percent real estate transfer fee when properties are sold; general revenues; voter-approved referenda in 1997, 1998, 2000, 2003, and 2008; grants; donations; and capital improve-ment project revenues.

"Reduction of traffic congestion and growth management are included in the criteria the Town Council uses to approve land acquisitions," Town Manager Steve Riley said in a March 2009 interview.

As the town celebrated its twenty-fifth anniversary of incorporation in 2008, Mayor Tom Peeples commented that people returning to Hilton Head Island after twenty years seemed pleased with what they found. "Our motto is 'Preserve and Prosper,' and I believe that falls true with the general attitude of the people of Hilton Head Island," he said. Peeples served on the Town Council that approved the first purchase of land for what became the Crossings Park, including the Bristol Sports Arena off Palmetto Bay Road.

The sixty-nine-acre Coastal Discovery Museum on the Honey Horn plantation is a joint venture with the town. Here visitors have an opportunity to step back in time and learn about the history and development of the island. In addition to a number of festivals, Honey Horn is the site of the annual Concours d'Elegance held on the first weekend in November. This event, which draws thousands to the island, features the showing and judging of vintage and antique automobiles.

The Volunteers in Medicine clinic, which opened in 1994, also stands on land the town purchased at Northridge and then leased for the clinic. The town later sold the parcel to VIM for one dollar so it could combine the land with other property it had purchased. Founded by Jack McConnell, M.D., with retired doctors, dentists, nurses, and others wanting to volunteer their services to those without medical care, VIM became a model for clinics established across the country.

On the north end of the island, Jarvis Creek Park has become a popular place for walkers, joggers, soccer enthusiasts, cookouts, and family outings. Created with two parcels totaling sixty-three acres, the park includes a freshwater pond stocked for catch-and-release fishing; a floating dock, with a reminder not to feed the alligators; a nature trail; paved pathways; grassy field; and a playground.

Jerry Barkie, who served as mayor from December 1989 to December 1991 recalled the efforts of the task force appointed to study the Nantucket Land Bank Program. He noted that Frank Chapman, who was a planner and later mayor, suggested this program as a model for Hilton Head. "I came from Long Island, New York, and the Long Island Expressway was known as the 'longest parking lot,'" Barkie said. "I didn't want to see Hilton Head become like that; so growth control was an important goal."

Walt Schymik headed the seven-member advisory Land Bank Commission that "went to school on the Nantucket Land Bank Program." This program, first of its kind in the U.S., receives two percent of the purchase price of Nantucket, Massachusetts, real estate for its fund.

The quarter-of-one-percent fee for Hilton Head Island property was a compromise approved by the Town Council in October 1990 after representatives of the real estate industry opposed a proposed one percent fee. Collections started in January 1991; and the town agreed to escrow the funds and test the authority of the ordinance to collect the Real Estate Transfer Fee, Riley said. Chester Williams, a local attorney who was planning to buy a home at the time, agreed to be the challenger. The town paid the legal bills.

The Supreme Court of South Carolina upheld the town's ordinance as "necessary and proper for the general welfare of the citizens of Hilton Head Island" in *Williams v. Town of Hilton Head Island.*

Meanwhile, Hilton Head's fee remains the only one of its kind in South Carolina. It was enacted three years prior to the General Assembly's adopting a code which forbids real estate transfer fees and taxes. The code grandfathered all such fees existing prior to January 1, 1991.

Schymik said commission members surveyed land about to be developed for land-banking possibilities and made recommendations to the Town Council. Following negotiations with developers and public hearings, council members voted on properties to be purchased for preservation or public uses. The town's staff eventually took over those responsibilities.

Recalling the months of research, local meetings, trips to Columbia to speak with state legislators, surveys, and the decision making process, Schymik said he thinks the program has gone well, "especially with Mayor Tom Peeples and Town Manager Steve Riley."

Information about the LMO or town-owned properties can be found through the subject index at www.hiltonheadislandsc.gov.

Photograph by Norma Van Amberg

Night Winds

by
Max D. Judge

Night winds carry images recalled in nostalgia
Of enchanting occasions gone by.
Echoes of laughter, sparkling cotillions
Are wafted by breezes on high.

Young lovers and friends in gowns and tuxedos
Are seen once again in the dark night.
Growing love, youthful passion, and tender embraces
Were thrilling adventures in moonlight.

Spirits of sharing sweet secrets of transport
Are mellow, enduring reflections.
Haunting refrains, night-walking ensembles
Cascade with gentle affection.

Fond mem'ries of romance and vibrant sensations
May be savored as lifetime extends.
Images and echoes are carried aloft
In zones of twilight by the night winds.

Mother Moon

by
Sharon Rice

On spare nights of dry-boned solitude
the gods—like young girls sprinkling rosebuds onto
        bridal paths—
come carrying baskets of moonlight.
Flung across the sky, the white seeps through my
        slatted window and comes to rest across my
        bedroom floor.

I rise, taking my blanket and pillow, and lie down in
        the arms of Mother Moon.
Outside, crickets cry and lightning bugs flash red and
        yellow,
And the wind moves among the ancient oaks, singing
        a lullaby.

Eve's Revenge

by
Sheila Gale

Eve stared at the knife stuck in Millie's heart. "Up to the hilt." The phrase had always seemed melodramatic. She had read something like it in one of her murder mysteries recently: "She plunged the knife so deeply that only the hilt was visible." Now Eve realized the words were an accurate description.

The deed had been much easier than she imagined. Millie had been in a deep sleep, and the knife slid between her ribs like soft cheese. Now, Millie, with her porcelain complexion and blonde hair, lay sprawled across the bed. Her mouth sagged open, and her baby-blue eyes stared out of an ashen face.

Eve trained the flashlight directly at Millie's unblinking eyes. "You don't look much like Miss Georgia Peach now."

Hands trembling, Eve fumbled in her pocket for a cigarette and, after several attempts, managed to light it. She stood by the open bedroom window, took a long drag, and exhaled from the side of her mouth. By the time she had finished the cigarette, the trembling had stopped. She flushed the butt down the toilet. Picking up Millie's air freshener, she sprayed the air a few times until all traces of smoke disappeared.

Eve rooted through Millie's jewelry box and stuffed necklaces, rings, and bracelets into a small knapsack she had picked up at Wal-Mart. Robbery often led to murder, didn't it? She hoped the police would see it that way. They did in mystery novels. To make it appear that the thief had been in a hurry, Eve left the lid open, dangled a necklace over the side of the box, and dropped a brooch onto the floor.

She crept downstairs. Millie's kitchen with its neat shelves, tidy countertops, and spotless floor had always impressed her. She had often teased her friend about being a neat freak. The flashlight's beam grazed over the butcher block, where knives were lined up in size order, ready to use, their steel blades glinting in the light. Eve stared at the space where the carving knife usually sat. Sometime during the next twenty-four hours that knife would be secured in a plastic bag by the police for evidence.

As she slipped out of the house, Eve smiled. Millie's habit of leaving the back door unlocked had served her well. She closed the door and glanced around. The only sounds came from the rustling of night creatures in the undergrowth. Car headlights flashed through the trees, illuminating the moonless night.

Eve removed the latex gloves and shoved them into the knapsack along with the flashlight and jewelry. She would get rid of the knapsack later. Retrieving her bike from behind some rhododendron bushes, she cycled home.

ഐ⁃ഐ⁃ഐ⁃ഐ⁃ഐ⁃ഐ⁃ഐ

Eve wheeled the bike into the garage. Her husband, Earl, had driven over to Savannah to visit his brother, so she would have the house to herself for a few hours. Shrouded in darkness, the house seemed cold and forbidding. Earl was never one to waste electricity. Well, stuff him! As she made her way to the den, Eve switched on every light. Removing her jacket, she dropped it on the sofa and flicked on the remote. CNN, what else? That was all Earl ever watched. She changed over to Fox and turned up the volume.

A half empty bottle of whiskey sat on the bar next to Earl's crystal hi-ball glass, one of a set she had given him on his sixtieth birthday. Every evening before dinner he poured himself a Scotch on the rocks. She picked up the glass. As she smoothed her fingers over the crystal, Eve's throat tightened. Swallowing hard, she rooted through his stash of booze for a bottle of rye and poured herself a healthy measure. She lifted the glass in a mock toast. "To Earl. May you suffer for the rest of your life for what you've done." Tears stung her eyes. She slammed the glass down on the bar counter so hard it splintered into pieces.

Damn you, Earl O'Malley! Damn you! Eve swept the shards of glass into the trash can and poured another drink. After several large sips, the tension in her body eased. From the ashtray on the table next to Earl's recliner, Eve picked up a half-smoked Gauloises. She lit the cigarette and settled back in the recliner. Friends teased her about her unusual taste in cigarettes. With all the American brands, why these? Eve had discovered the pungent French cigarettes in her early twenties when she traveled through Europe to celebrate graduation from law school. She had been smoking them for almost forty years now and was not about to change brands at this stage of her life.

Earl did not approve of Eve's smoking and could not stand the Gauloises cigarettes. "They stink, and they're full of tar. I'm warning you, Eve, those cigarettes will be your downfall."

Eve knew how to shut Earl up. "And what about your drinking! That's not doing your liver any good."

She inhaled, holding her breath for a few seconds before blowing out a long stream of smoke.

They had married young, and together they had built up a successful business, O'Malley's Furniture Inc. Eve, with her sharp features and sallow skin, was no beauty; and she had known right from the start that, with his lazy smile and deep blue eyes, Earl attracted women. Though she only worked part time at O'Malley's, Eve kept a keen lookout for any female employee who cast her eyes in his direction. She was O'Malley's legal advisor but also hired the office staff. That Lily, with her swaying hips and curly blonde hair, had thought she was a shoo-in for the receptionist's position; but Eve offered the job to a middle-aged matron with legs like tree trunks. And what about that Mandy Danson, from Accounts! Just by chance, Eve had dropped by Earl's office one day to find her leaning over his desk, boobs spilling out of a lime green spandex top tucked into a skirt so short it left nothing to the imagination. Mandy had left O'Malley's the next day, telling everyone she had been offered a better job. Only Eve knew the truth.

A few years ago, when Earl was fifty-eight, she had watched in horror as he clutched his chest and collapsed on the bedroom floor. After the heart attack, he sank into a deep depression. He refused to seek help and began to drink heavily, often arriving home after midnight, a bottle of booze in his hand, reeking of whiskey and cheap perfume. One night he staggered into the house, his arm slung around a slightly-built Asian woman. "This, this is . . . Crystal," he had slurred, trying to focus his bloodshot eyes on Eve. "She's from China."

Eve had marched into the kitchen, filled a pot with cold water, and threw it over them. "Get out!" she screamed. She picked up an ornate vase that Earl had given her for their twenty-fifth wedding anniversary and threw it at him. It missed and smashed onto the stone tiles. As she stared at the broken pieces, Eve decided she had had enough of Earl's shenanigans. Early next morning, she had called a locksmith to change the locks.

Free to do as she pleased, Eve took ballroom dancing lessons, joined a book club, and signed up for Italian classes. An avid reader, she enjoyed a wide selection of topics, including murder mysteries. Her busy life kept her well occupied; but in the evenings, when the grandfather clock in the hall chimed six, she found herself listening for Earl's key in the lock and his booming voice calling out to see if she was home. He would stride across the living room and give her a kiss. "Hi, Teach." His nickname for her stemmed from high school days, when she had tutored him in math.

A year after they had separated, the doorbell rang. Leaving the chain on, Eve opened the door just enough to see who had dropped by. Earl stood on the porch. Even with his thinning hair and a bit of a paunch, he looked dapper in a navy blue blazer and beige chinos. He held a large bouquet of red roses in his arms. Eve's heart began to flutter as she remembered the night Earl proposed to her. He had sworn his undying love and presented her with a red rose.

Telling herself not to be sentimental, Eve opened the door.

He shuffled his feet. "Eve, I've come to beg you to take me back."

"After the way you treated me? You must be kidding!"

His face grew pale. "Look, I know I behaved badly, but could you try to forgive me?" His eyes pleaded with her.

Eve said nothing.

"I sold the business. I want you to come with me to Hilton Head. We can buy a house and retire there."

"You expect me to drop everything, just like that?"

"It's a bit sudden, I know . . ."

Eve cut in. "Do you realize what you did to me, with all your drinking and womanizing!"

Earl hung his head. "I love you, Eve. I'll never hurt you again. I know I can't take back the pain I've caused you, but will you give me another chance?"

"I'll think about it."

As he handed her the flowers, his voice cracked. "Don't take too long."

After Earl drove away, Eve made a pot of coffee. Settling down in her favorite chair, she sipped the hot drink and mulled over everything he had said. Her heart told her to give him another chance, but could he be trusted? Closing her eyes, she breathed in the roses' heady perfume and came to a decision. She would go to South Carolina with him and give their marriage another try.

Six months later they drove down to Hilton Head and bought a house in Sea Pines. Eve's dream of an idyllic retirement had come true. She pushed all the unhappy memories to the back of her mind and threw herself into island life. They played golf twice a week, took long bike rides through shaded plantations, and dined out with new-found friends. They lounged on their deck on hot, sultry afternoons drinking iced tea. Sometimes they would take a picnic and enjoy a lazy afternoon on the beach.

She met Millie, a widow from nearby Georgia, at the local tennis club shortly after arriving on Hilton Head; and they became close friends. After their weekly tennis match the two women would go back to either Eve or Millie's house for coffee and catch up on the latest gossip.

The dream had lasted for three years. It began to unravel a month ago when Eve, sorting out the laundry, discovered a lipstick stain on Earl's shirt. She sniffed the shirt. Flowery perfume! She rummaged through his trousers and jackets. Nothing. Eve remembered he had been wearing blue jeans lately. The pockets were empty, except for a piece of scrunched-up paper lodged in the corner of a back pocket. Eve smoothed it out and saw a phone number scrawled in turquoise ink. Heart racing, she had punched in the number.

It rang three times before an answering machine kicked in. "Hi, this is Millie. I can't come to the phone right now. Please leave a message."

Eve felt the blood drain from her face. It was her friend Millie's voice, but it wasn't her phone number. Surely there must be a mistake! Then Eve remembered that Millie had bought a cell phone a few weeks ago.

She sank onto the bed, numb with shock. Her best friend, Millie, and her husband, Earl, were having an affair!

After a while the numbness had disappeared, and anger bubbled up inside her. How could they do this to her! Why hadn't she realized what was going on? Earl's sudden interest in bridge should have been a red flag. Bridge! Hah! He had been meeting Millie. She had been widowed for two years and lived alone in that big house. Set back from the road and almost hidden by trees, it was ideal for a liaison. And what about that diet Earl went on a few months ago? He always claimed diets were a waste of time, so she should have been suspicious of his new-found enthusiasm for vegetables and yogurt. What a fool she had been. And that two-faced so-called friend of hers! How could she have sex with Earl one day and meet Eve for lunch the next?

Eve felt weary all of a sudden. She drained the glass. Time for one more smoke, then bed. She searched around for another pack of cigarettes but could not find any. What about the pack she had taken with her to Millie's house? She picked up the discarded jacket and searched though the pockets. All she found were tissues and candy wrappers.

The shrill ring of the phone made her jump. She picked up the receiver. "Hello?"

"Hi, honey. It's Earl."

Her grip tightened. "Where are you?"

"About to turn into Millie's driveway."

"What are you doing there?"

"Whoa—what's up with you? Millie and I have been roped into organizing the annual bridge tournament—remember? I told you about it the other day."

"It's nine thirty."

"I know. She's gonna hand me a list of names then I'll be outta here." He sighed. "I'm beat. That brother of mine is hard going sometimes. Anyway, I'll see you in a couple minutes."

"How could you do this to me!" A sob caught in Eve's throat. "You and Millie . . ."

"Honey, have you been drinkin' or somethin'? What are you talkin' about?"

"It's no use denying it, Earl. I found lipstick stains on your shirt. It reeked of perfume. And I found the number of Millie's cell phone in your jeans pocket."

"Jeez, Eve. I'm sorry. I shoulda told you." He paused. "Remember a few weeks ago when I won the Island Classic Golf Tournament? They had these young women— sort-a like cheerleaders—to hand out the prizes. They kissed the guys and made a fuss because the *Island Packet* wanted photos." He paused. "I promised you I'd never hurt you again. I meant it then, and I mean it now. I love you, Eve." He laughed. "Even though you do smoke those goddamned Gauloises cigarettes!"

It all came rushing back. On her way to collect the air freshener from the bathroom, she had left the packet of cigarettes on Millie's dressing table.

Earl had warned her those cigarettes would be her downfall.

North toward Home

by
Frederick W. Bassett

Southern-born and reared, you could swap
story for story with any native son.
My favorite is of you as a little girl
digging for the bones of Jesus
in a churchyard near your grandmother's farm.
But you were as misplaced there
as with your mother in segregated Wilmington.
Ah, but all those afternoon movies—
solace for a Don Juan father long gone,
and wings to soar above the hours.
Then that dashing young artist from Syracuse
came braving a southern college.
No way his double-plated armor
could withstand your fierce passion.
So you won the skirmish in North Carolina
only to lose the war in New York.
O Catherine, how life ticks down
role by role—young mother, divorcee,
paramour, television star, professor—
and now the long shadows fall.
There is no script. What can I say?
You are the novel I wish I could write.

for Catherine Marlowe Hawkins

Fickle

by
Art Cornell

The bumble bee
Staggers from the rose
Only to be captivated
By the daffodil.

Striving

by
Art Cornell

Wings beating
Furiously to reach
The sweetest nectar;
Much like man
Is the hummingbird.

Poems Written While in Japan

by
Norm Levy

Carefully inscribed on rice paper squares
A cascade of secret wishes
Flutter down from mountain heights
Into a crystal stream a thousand feet below.
Only one is seized by a playful breeze
And vaulted toward the clouds—out of sight.
Is it mine?

↔↔↔↔↔

A dusty tongue,
A rusty beard,
And hollow echoes of half-remembered laughter
Are all that remain from a long night of drinking.
I am unwell.

↔↔↔↔↔

Despite the sun's warmth
The air is icy.
My shadow—naked and unprotected
Freezes fast—unable to follow.
I hurry on—alone.

From the yellowed, ancient leaves
Of a holy chronicle
A shiny black roach scurries out
To seize a tiny crumb
Fallen from the sleeve of a prayerful pilgrim.

↔↔↔↔↔

The grass is more enduring
Than the stone fortresses of warriors.
When mighty battlements crumble into
    pebbles and shards
Blades of grass, not of steel, will protect the ruins
From the contemptuous glances of strangers.

Pauline

by
Sharon Rice

Pauline
stands under the purple street light,
her white starched collar stiff against the nape of her neck—
upturned in the style of the late 1950s.

Her head tilts back, and her mouth opens,
laughter flowing out into the summer twilight—
music as round and pealing as her voice singing on Sunday mornings.
I watch her hands move to lift her hair away from the collar,
hands that hold me transfixed
as they move across piano keys
or touch my elder sister's hair in affection.

On the cool outer steps of the church
I watch the older children as they
run and play hide-and-seek in the dark.
I sit in the shadow of the great stone building
watching Pauline, a goddess bathed in purple light.

Lobster Love

by
Charlie McOuat

"Aw, damn, I'm trapped!"

My feelers undulated between the wooden slats; my claws ripped at the nylon netting; my tail flapped in the mud. Nothing helped. The cod head that I had chewed on an hour ago was reeking. "I'm stewed," was all I could say. I struggled, cursed some more, then made a deal with God that if He chose to get me out of this mess, I would change my ways. No more being controlled by passions. Eating and sex had been my weaknesses, and now I needed His help.

Suddenly the whole world started shaking. I was being lifted from my familiar mud up towards the surface where I had not been since I was a larva, twelve years before. "Good bye, Cape Cod Bay," was the last thing I remember saying before being hauled out of the water onto that filthy boat where they stuck those wooden pegs in my carapace. I was completely helpless. They threw me on the ice and hauled me on that hour truck ride over the bumpy beach to the market. I knew my life had changed forever.

That was two months ago. That night I was airlifted to Florida. For three weeks I rested in one of those glass cages with Larry, Leroy, Lolita, and Louise. All those damned humans were staring at us. The worst were the kids tapping on the glass. I would have liked to have gotten one those little brats in the water with me and seen how smart they would be then.

Larry disappeared first. Two big human hands came and lifted him out. We never saw him again. Leroy and Louise went together; then it was just Lolita and me.

Me? Oh, sorry, I'm Louis, Louis the Lobster. Sorry I took so long to introduce myself. My roommate was Lolita—definitely not my type. Her tail was too small. And huge claws. I could not get near her if I wanted to. And what a personality! So-o aggressive and nasty. I was afraid to go to sleep. Afraid she might eat me.

I was almost relieved when a few days later those same hairy hands grabbed me, put me on the scale, stuffed me in a paper bag, and jammed me into that ice chest. He carried me aboard his yacht like I was a piece of meat. The guy had no respect.

"We're sailin' out to the Keys," he said to someone. "The Keys," he repeated. "We're sailin' out to the Keys."

What the hell are the Keys? I wondered. It does not matter. He had one of those long-haired humans with him. One of those things that talks so sweet and sashays around like she was a queen. But hey. No distractions. Not this time. They were drinking and carrying on, propagating their species something fierce. They got that yacht really rocking. But I knew I had to concentrate. This was serious.

Despite everything, it was great to be back at sea. I felt better. I liked that rocking and rolling of the boat, almost like home. I felt the change in the air. I was energized, confident, borderline cocky even.

I've got one chance, I said to myself, *One chance and that's it. When that drunken lover boy lays a hand on me, he's going to get one giant pinch on the face. He'll feel pain like he's never felt before. I've got to do it right-clawed. It's the only one I could free from that awful peg. A horrendous pinch; and hopefully he'll be so angry, he'll howl and panic and throw me overboard. I'll be free.*

A long shot, sure, but it was all I could think of at the time. Here is what happened.

Things got serious really fast. When he lifted me from the bag, I saw daylight, reached out, and grabbed his red, obnoxious, bulbous nose. I squeezed hard; and, miracle of miracles, he yelped and fell forward onto the guard rail. The momentum hurled us both into the sea. He belched, burped, and puked. I let go his nose and swam like mad. I never want to see him again. Ever.

O-w-w! I just hit bottom. This is not soft mud like Cape Cod Bay. This is hard sand and rocks and corals and clear water. I can see twenty feet away. It is beautiful down here, with all those pretty colors, but hot. I just feel like going to sleep. Even that glass tank was cooler than this, but it is so-o-o pretty. Yellow, purple, and red coral—I have never seen anything like this. Those prickly, black sea urchins look mean, though. I want no part of them. And those barracuda, such sharp teeth. I have to watch my butt around here.

But wow! What do we have here? All pink and pretty, and a huge tail flapping at me so nice. And look! No claws. She is CUTE, and I mean cute. A lobster with a huge tail and no claws. And she sees me. Here she comes.

Oh, now I have it. That incident with the trap, the pegs, and the glass case. That was my passage. I am cooked, no, not cooked. Bad expression. I am dead. Real dead, and this is heaven. This is it, I know it is. Heaven. The coral, the warmer water, the slower pace; and now best of all, this ravishing babe with gorgeous eyes, sexy tail, and no claws is coming on to me.

"Hi there, handsome," she says in that slow Southern drawl while twitching her protruding eyes, "I'm Lola. I haven't seen you around before. Do you come here often, big boy? Where have you been all my life? Where have you been hidin', you macho guy, you. And look at those claws. I'd like to have them wrapped around me some night. I'm smitten."

Well, that is the end of my freedom. I take one look at her, and I am trapped by her seductiveness. Now I am a prisoner of love. Lobster love. A victim of my own desires, just as helpless as being in that cage. But I admit, it is a lot better here with Lola than in that cage. There just is no comparison.

"I'm coming, dear. Sorry to keep you waiting. And of course, darling, I'll even shed my carapace for you. Any day, all day, any time. Yes, you're right, dear, I will be more careful with my claws. Yes, dear. Sorry, dear, I'm coming."

Osprey

Photograph by Sansing McPherson

Hilton Head Sunset

Photograph by Art Cornell

Saw Palmetto

Photograph by Sansing McPherson

Egret

Photograph by Linda Benning

Baby Alligator

Photograph by Sansing McPherson

Kayakers

Photograph by Art Cornell

Shrimp Boats

Photograph by Roger Benning

Sunrise over Port Royal Sound

Photograph by Sansing McPherson

The Tryst

by
C. S. Thorn, Jr.

Her e-mail was brief and to the point. "Darling Mario, Reggie will be gone for a week. Please come to me on Thursday. I can feel your body next to mine already. Love, S."

The breeze that rattled the sea grapes earlier had softened to a whisper, barely audible above the soughing of the surf. The last of the sun's rays streamed from the west and peeked around the multi-million dollar mansions crowded together at the ocean's edge. The daily throng of beach goers had decamped, and in the flagging light the silhouettes of two ships bound for Port Everglades glided across the horizon to the east.

Miguel and Maria Cordoza had finished their chores. They were having supper in the downstairs kitchen as they watched *Dr. Phil* on a small TV perched atop a baker's rack.

Maria had greeted Señora Gillespie at the door when she returned home half an hour earlier. Serena had stayed too long at lunch with a friend, and Maria assumed she had had too much wine. But the young woman seemed alert, and her words were not slurred.

"Maria, I am having friends over later. I won't need any help. You and Miguel might like to visit with your sister. You may leave whenever you wish."

"Ah, Señora, *con gusto*. I have not seen my sister in such a long time. *Gracias*, we will leave after supper."

Serena mounted the stairs and went straight to her room. She discarded her clothes in a trail across the tiled floor before making her preparations. The beach in front of the house was now empty and dark, and only the lights of the ships were visible. Minutes later the form of a lovely woman could be seen from the balcony lying on a huge, canopied bed. Blonde hair framed her exquisite features as sheer curtains billowed in the air drifting through the open doors.

He had received her e-mail but did not respond. He would go to Serena, he decided; but he would surprise her. Mario Pegano would climb to her balcony as he had done before. The Cordozas would never know he was there. He became aroused as he thought of her alabaster skin contrasting with the bronze of his own. He wondered if she would be napping as was her habit in the early evening. He would wake her with a kiss.

On Thursday afternoon he crossed the Intracoastal Waterway, pulled the flame-red Porsche Carrera up in front of The Breakers, and handed the keys to a parking valet. He wore a pale coral silk shirt and beige linen Ralph Lauren slacks that had been gifts from Valerie Carson, who also owned the Porsche. He walked through the lobby, exiting through a rear door to a shallow lawn protected from the surf by a bulkhead. Following the grass to the southeast corner of the property, he made his way to the beach. He carried his Gucci loafers in one hand and trudged through the soft sand to the big home on South County Road. She would be waiting for him. He knew she would.

When Reggie Gillespie was away, he called Miguel or Maria between five and six every day to confirm that Serena was home; but rarely did he ask to speak with her. The Cordozas were very loyal, perhaps because of the extra $1,000 he paid them in cash every month. This day he had called just as they were finishing supper.

"Hello, Maria. How is everything?"

"Ah, Señor Gillespie, *buenos diás*. The Señora is home, and she is resting in her room."

"That's fine, Maria. I will be home tomorrow, and I will see you then."

"*Si, Señor. Adiós, véale mañana.*"

౿౿౿౿౿౿౿౿౿

Mario's pace slackened as he neared the big house. He climbed the dune and looked all around. Satisfied there was no one about, he crept around the pool and the hot tub and moved into the shadows under the balcony. Pausing for a minute, he listened. The only sound was the splashing of water from the fountain. Satisfied that he had not been seen, he slipped his bare feet into his shoes before climbing the trellis. Once at the top he stopped again. As before, all was quiet. He stepped over the balustrade to the balcony.

He opened two more buttons on the front of his shirt, exposing the gold chain Serena had given him. He slicked back his hair and moved to the open door to look inside. The sheet had fallen away exposing her to the waist. In the dim light he could see only the left side of her face and the provocative curve of her breasts, but he knew she was stunningly beautiful.

He was about to step through the curtains when he sensed movement near the door at the far corner of the room. Turning his head imperceptibly, he squinted for a better look. Someone was moving very slowly. An arm drew back, and he heard a metallic *twang*, followed by a *thunk*.

His eyes moved back to Serena. Six inches of a feathered arrow protruded from her bosom. Mario froze. He looked back to the dark corner, but it was empty. He did not run to Serena or call for help. He did what came most naturally. He fled.

He climbed frantically back down the trellis, jumping when he was six feet off the ground. He fell to his knees, but when he stood up to run something slammed into the back of his head. Everything went black.

જ⁓જ⁓જ⁓જ⁓જ

When Mario next opened his eyes, someone was rifling his pockets. A crusty substance clung to the man's scraggly whiskers, and his clothes exuded a noisome odor. Mario jerked away. It was early morning, and he was lying on concrete in some sort of an alley with the worst headache of his life.

"Get the hell away from me. Move, or I'll call the police."

The man laughed. "Ain't no cops 'round here. Dey don't come in dis neighborhood."

"What are you talking about? Where am I?" Mario looked around and noticed broken bottles, empty trash cans, and all manner of debris.

"You in a alley. Cain't you see dat?"

"No, I mean what part of town is this?"

"Dis is de shit part of town, sonny."

He tried to sit up, but his neck and the back of his head were throbbing. He felt behind his head and discovered a lump at the base of his skull. "How long have I been here?"

"Beats me, I got here two minutes ago. I thought you was dead."

Mario got unsteadily to his feet. "How do I get out of here?"

"You wanna borrow my Mercedes?" The man pointed to his battered shopping cart and cackled.

Mario walked through a wasteland for twenty minutes before he found a main street. When he was finally able to flag a cab, he flopped into the rear seat.

"Where to?" asked the driver.

"The Breakers."

"The what?"

"The Breakers," Mario repeated, "on Royal Poinciana."

"Where the hell is that?"

"On the ocean in Palm Beach. Are you new here?"

"Palm Beach? Mister, you in Miami. What the hell do I know about Palm Beach?"

Mario was dumbfounded. "Well, I need to go to Palm Beach. Will you take me?"

"Sure, if you got the jack. That'll be a hundred bucks in advance."

"Okay, okay." But a flash of panic crossed Mario's face as he discovered the comforting bulge behind his left hip was missing. "Oh my God, they stole my wallet."

"Yeah, right. Okay, get outta my cab."

"No, wait. I've got the money." Mario pulled off his belt and unzipped a hidden compartment. He extracted two fifty-dollar bills and handed them to the cabbie.

"Okay, let's go."

His mind raced as he thought about the events of the night before. Was it Reggie Gillespie who sapped him? How did he get to Miami? And if Serena had been killed, why was he still alive?

ৡ৽ৡ৽ৡ৽ৡ৽ৡ৽

An hour later when he stepped out of the taxi at The Breakers, the valet raised his eyebrows and eyed the filthy clothes. Mario explained that he had been mugged and that the parking stub had disappeared along with his stolen wallet.

"Just a minute, sir." The valet reached for a portable phone. He dialed a number and walked a few steps away, speaking quietly before returning to the stand. "My supervisor will be out right away."

A nervous-looking manager appeared immediately and introduced himself. As Mario explained his predicament, a police cruiser pulled silently into the breezeway. Two uniformed cops got out and approached him from behind.

"Is this him?" the bigger one asked the manager. The man was obviously relieved and managed to nod his head in the affirmative.

"Mr. Pegano, you're under arrest. Put your arms out behind you, please."

"What's this all about? I . . ."

"Now, Mr. Pegano," snapped the cop. "Let's do this the easy way."

Uncomprehending, Mario extended his arms backward as the officer slipped on the handcuffs and read him his Miranda rights. The cops led him to the cruiser and eased him into the back seat.

"Please tell me what this is all about. I just came by to pick up my car."

"Your car? You mean the red Porsche? That car is registered to a Valerie Carson."

"Well, she let's me use it."

"Is that why you murdered her?"

Mario was dumbstruck. He felt pounding in his heart and a loosening in his bowels. For a few seconds he thought he might faint. "Murdered?" he blurted. "What do you mean? I saw her on Monday, and she was fine."

"Well, she's not fine now. She's down at the morgue with a nasty arrow sticking out of her; and, oh yeah, we found the cross bow, too. It's got your prints all over it."

"No, no. You've got it wrong. Valerie's not dead. It was Serena who was killed. I saw it happen, but I didn't do it."

The cops looked at each other. One said, "I thought we'd heard it all before, but this is a new twist. The perp claims the stiff is someone else."

His partner replied, "Well, Homicide can sort it out. All we got to do is book him."

"Yeah, well, I'm starvin' here, Pete. By the time we run him in and finish the paperwork, it will be two thirty or three. We gotta stop and get some lunch."

"I'm with you. What about the McDonald's on Federal?"

"Good idea. I'll sit with him at one of those outside tables, and you go in. I'll take a Big Mac, a Coke, and two orders of fries with extra grease."

The patrol car eased into McDonald's back parking area and stopped in front of a pair of picnic tables next to a dumpster enclosure and the side wall of an adjacent building. There they would be shielded from the view of any curious onlookers. The big cop, who was driving, got out and opened the rear door.

"Okay, Pegano, we're gonna have a picnic. Take a seat right there." He pointed to the side of a table facing away from the parking area. Handing his partner some cash, he said, "Hurry it up, Pete, before I faint from hunger."

He took a seat across the table from Mario and smiled at him. "A pretty boy like you will be real popular in the joint. In fact, they're gonna love you."

He was overweight, and his red face seemed to turn purple as he laughed. He was so taken with his joke that he continued to chortle, but suddenly his expression changed. His smile gave way to a grimace, and he began to cough. He reached for his chest and throat and struggled to inhale. There was fear in his wide-open eyes as he gasped and collapsed on the table.

Mario could not believe his good fortune. He was no doctor, but he would bet that he had just witnessed a fatal heart attack. He waited a minute longer before springing up and rushing around the table. With his arms secured behind him it was awkward, but Mario searched the cop's pockets for the key to the handcuffs. It was not there. In desperation he crossed to the patrol car and looked through the still-open front door. The key sat on the caddy between the seats. He had to hurry. He backed into the car and sat sideways, feeling behind him. He grasped the key in one hand and felt for the keyhole with the tips of his fingers. Seconds later his left hand was free, and then he wrenched his right hand loose. He left the cuffs in plain sight on the console.

But he could not risk fleeing the parking lot. Pete would be back any second. Mario noticed a narrow opening behind the dumpster that was just wide enough for his small frame. He squeezed into it. He hoped it would appear that he was long gone, and he waited in his foul-smelling hideaway as the other cop returned.

When Pete discovered his partner face down on the table, he shouted into the radio. In minutes an ambulance arrived, and the big cop's body was removed. Pete departed in the cruiser, and for the moment Mario was safe. If he could remain undiscovered until dark, he would make his way across town to the rail yard and hop a northbound freight to Jacksonville. From there he could connect with CSX or Norfolk Southern to any part of the country. He was familiar with this mode of travel. It had brought him to Florida in the first place.

One thing was certain. He would never voluntarily return to the Sunshine State. Mario had been busted for minor offenses in the past: trafficking in stolen goods and a couple of drug raps. But this was murder—a double murder; or so it sounded. He would have to disappear.

૭ઃ૭ઃ૭ઃ૭ઃ૭ઃ૭ઃ

A few blocks away Pete pulled the cruiser up behind the ambulance. The big cop stepped out. "I'm feeling better already."

They exchanged a laugh.

"You should have seen his face when I told him they were gonna love him in the joint. I bet he'll be five hundred miles away by tomorrow."

Pete said, "You never told me how you got involved in this."

"Well, sometimes I work for the Gillespie woman on the side. When she has a party, I handle the parking, you know, things like that. Anyway, she and her friend are having lunch and swapping tales; and they discover that that this Pegano guy is two-timing them. One describes a gold chain she gave him, and the other one remembers seeing him wear it."

"They call me on my cell phone, and I meet them at the restaurant. They want to teach the guy a lesson, and I get the idea from a movie I seen. All we need is a mannequin, and it turns out Gillespie already has one of herself. They make her dresses on it or something. We put a blond wig on the damn thing. Bingo, it looks just like her, especially in a dark room. I enlist an old friend who has a crossbow, and we're all set. Of course I had to give our boy a lift to Miami. I thought that would be the end of him, but when he came to get the Porsche, I realized he needed a little more encouragement."

Pete smiled. "I'm sorry I missed the first part. By the way, here's your Big Mac and fries."

The big cop stuffed the food into a nearby trash container.

"Pete, you aren't serious, are you? That stuff will kill you."

Crows

by
Frederick W. Bassett

They said my father, as a boy, tamed a crow.
It slept on a perch in his room
then circled with him during the day.
In time, it circled wider and wider
until it didn't need the boy nor he the crow.
Yesterday, I watched a flock of them
swarming after a red-tailed hawk
that winged its way, almost casually,
toward some distant perch, belly stuffed
with the warm flesh of their nestlings.
Soaring, diving, they buzzed the hawk
as though they were winning the battle.
This morning, it was a marauding
crow that did the taking, as slender
mockingbirds, mismatched except for pluck,
fought the same losing battle.
I mused on that irony until black-feathered
melancholy swooped me away.
I'm scaling a long-leaf pine
that stretches straight into the sky
for forty feet before branching out
to host a nest of baby crows. I bundle one
in my shirt and slide down the swaying pine.
It was mostly stomach with a wide,
wobbly throat that I assumed
could feed itself like any newborn chicken.

Crows

I did my part, I thought, littering
the cardboard box with worms, crickets,
even chicken mash in desperation.
Across the years, I've kept a special eye
for crows, and sometimes I fly with them,
winging time until I'm a boy,
standing in the shadow of my tall father.

Funny Money

by
Norm Levy

Markets Have a Funny Way Of Reacting to Reality Once They Think It Through

The New York Times: January 14, 1999
(A quote in an article on economic turmoil)

A market that can "think it through"!

I've never met one, think, have you?

A market can at times be funny.

I've seen one laugh—then eat my money!

If markets really think at all

They know two things: to rise . . . then F
A
L
L

A Scent of Lilac

by
Sharon Rice

When I was ten, my father gave me an orphaned pup to care for. Not to my older brother or sister, but to me because he knew me. I named her Bandit for the obvious reason of the patch of color surrounding each eye. On the first night she was with me, I took her into my bed because I couldn't bear her orphan cries—though I had been strongly warned against doing any such thing by my mama. From that point on, Bandit became my steadfast companion.

I think she knew we were kin in some way and could remember those nights soon after her mama died when I would rise from my bed and sneak out into the kitchen. I would lift her out of the cardboard box next to the coal oil stove and take her back to my room. After I nuzzled all my secrets into her soft ears, she would sleep the rest of the night curled up against my stomach.

It was a game we played, my mama and I. She would wake me every morning and find that sweet bandit-faced pup somewhere in my bed. She never spoke a word then, but every night she would say to me, "Sarabeth, don't you go putting that dirty dog in on my sheets, you hear?" Strange what proprietary instincts mothers have about the oddest things: "Don't be walking with those muddy shoes on my clean kitchen floor, you hear?" Or: "Don't you be messing up my clean front room." Maybe it's because they don't have much else to claim—no fancy diamonds or furs.

We played that game for two weeks, but I won. Mama didn't really have a chance, endurance being a primal tactic of all children everywhere. My persistent disobedience outlasted my mama's warnings—and her time and energy. Pretty soon her mind became too distracted by other cares of the household, so Bandit stayed in my bed at night until her own need for independence outweighed my need to give comfort.

Our connection continued during those years I lived in the house on the corner—kitty corner, as they say—from the Sohio filling station that stood on the edge of our small town. The station stood in the middle of the Y where Main Street branched off into two directions out of town. Leaning toward the left led you to Millionaire's Row—a new section of ranch-style homes built on the outskirts by blue-collar workers who had borrowed from the Devil in order to stand apart from the rest of us. Leaning toward the right led nowhere in particular except to the farm of a family who attended the Baptist Church in town. Our house, one of a series of rented homes, sat at the edge of the Y that leaned right.

During those years on that corner, I spent many hours sitting on the wrap-around porch watching the world go by. Bandit sat there, right next to me, licking my face and whining in commiseration over the normal adolescent woes. From time to time she would pick herself up, stretch long and slowly, and then lumber off to the lilac bush close by to do her business.

One July afternoon we were sitting in the corner of the porch shaded by the old oak tree, trying to be as cool as possible in the heat and humidity of summer in the Ohio Valley. Some parts of the porch were rough and grainy, but this one in the corner was as slick and cool as glass. I was off some place deep in my mind. Bandit was lying there next to me, her pink tongue hanging loose out of her mouth and her tiny body panting to try its own good best to keep cool.

It was the still part of the day, five thirty or so. Still, as in almost everybody was at home eating dinner. Still, as in that time of day in the summer when no breath of air was stirring, not even a leaf. But within one split second all hell broke loose. Sounds were sucked up together into one and then separated out again into squealing tires, a dull thud, and screaming human voices. Later I would imagine one had been mine.

Doors along the street opened, and neighbors poured out like hot milk bubbling over the rim of the pan. No one emerged from our door as Mama and Daddy both were still at work and my truant siblings were still scattered at play. As usual, I was the solitary witness for our household of what went on in the street in front of our house. My mind cleared enough to try to put names to faces, but there were two I couldn't see: the one who had been driving and the one I knew had to be lying there on the ground hidden from me by the human circle.

To this day there are things I still don't know. Like how something so terrible could appear from the universe and land on the street in front of me. And whether anyone took any notice that I was even there. But there Bandit and I sat, peering through the white wooden slats of the railing. Me, afraid to breathe.

Within minutes the sound of the police cruisers, looming shadows in reverse, broke the silence before I actually saw them. They finally pulled up to the curb. The ambulance would take another ten minutes or so since we didn't have our own and had to call for one from nearby Feesburg. We didn't know it then, but it was already too late. Too late, as in that terrible place of living in a reality that has already passed. Like when you're still loving and trusting somebody who's already left without your knowing it. Or sending a letter to your dear friend, only to find out they were dead when you wrote it.

I moved down to the other end of the porch to get a better look. Now I was barely twenty-five feet from the curb. I could see my neighbors' faces, frozen in unreleased horror. From time to time a wail cut through the air.

The door to the car opened, and I could see a man lying inside, flung across the seat. I could hear him weeping, like I'd never heard another human weep, except maybe in my own mind. Deep, wrenching sobs. Somebody approached him from the other side of the car, and he tried to raise himself up. When he did, I saw a face I'd seen every weekday for the last year.

The previous summer, Mr. Kearns had moved with his family to our town to become the new principal of our school. He was tall, burly, and balding, with a hot temper and scowl to match. I had been afraid of Mr. Kearns ever since the first day I had laid eyes on him in the seventh grade. It wasn't until years later that I realized I shouldn't have taken his scowl so personally. But back then I just knew he creased that high forehead purposefully in my direction. Of course, it didn't help that out of school I would see him smoking a cigar. Or that everybody in town knew where he was, or wasn't, on a Sunday morning.

But the day I saw Mr. Kearns lift himself up out of the seat, two things happened: a welling-up of compassion replaced my fear of him, and my heart aged with the weight of the loss of Eden's innocence. Without anybody telling me, I knew Mr. Kearns's life had changed forever. Somehow I knew he was wishing it were his own body they were lifting up off the road and putting inside the ambulance. And I also believed that even if his name would be cleared of any blame, he would carry a seal—invisible to an outsider's eye—as heavy as any yellow arm band or scarlet A. And what would be most terrible is that he would be the one who gouged it into his own forehead: "Damned." Damned to carry the burden of his own living, his own continued existence.

The next month, in August—a week before I was to enter eighth grade—Mr. Kearns and his family moved away.

As for Bandit and me, we continued our vigil. During the day, I was off at school, hurrying through the hours so I could get home again. But at night, life was slow and easy as we watched the cars lean left or right out of town. Not much happened. One late October afternoon we did see Mr. Harley James, fodder for the town gossips, in his faded blue pickup chasing after Mabel—her chemically-induced strawberry-blond hair leaving wispy streaks of sunset as she blazed out of town in her daddy's new white convertible. No doubt, it was another case of her deciding to leave Harley for good.

As we sat there in the dusk that fell like new smoke, Bandit stood, stretched her spotted body, and then lumbered off toward the lilac bush. I was left wondering where Mabel might be off to. Perhaps she was going back to her mama and daddy who were sitting and waiting for their dear girl to come home. Ready with her room that had not changed one bit since she left two years earlier. According to those gossips, at seventeen she had walked out of her parents' home to join her life with Harley, leaving her red and white cheerleading uniform flung across a chair and no promise of a white wedding gown in her future. Or maybe she was off to see some new young man who held out even greater promises than Harley had proven to offer.

Bandit's wet nose nudged at my elbow. Dark had settled around us, a sure signal to go in for supper. These days "supper" meant no mama. Working the night shift, she would be standing even now sorting soup can labels to earn money for our family. Bandit was allowed to lie on the kitchen floor while I heated up the meal Mama had prepared for us. For the last several years, though, we had followed Mama's new rule that Bandit had to sleep on the porch.

At nine o'clock, I called Bandit's name. Eyelids barely lifted in her sleep, so I scooped her up and carried her out to the porch steps where we sat under the stars, me wishing my mama were home to ease the end of my day into sleep. But it was Bandit's body that shielded me from the autumn night air, and her slow breathing that softened my lonely heart.

Because my mama slept while I was at school, I did not see her the next morning either. Instead, Bandit jumped and licked every inch of skin she could find in farewell. I laughed as I realized her salutations and benedictions were interchangeable.

When I came into the house that Thursday afternoon, I lay my books on the round wooden kitchen table given to us by my maternal grandmother. I turned to call Bandit's name out the screen door, and in the same instance realized that my mama was home. I could hear her voice, quiet and blurred, in the next room.

I shivered. My mama was rarely home when I returned from school. And when she was there, she was never just sitting. She was hanging up or taking down t-shirts, towels, and sheets from the clothesline. Or flinging her voice throughout the house, chiding one of us about something we had or had not done.

But that day she was sitting in the living room on our blue sofa.

My legs turned heavy. I knew that when I walked into that room, I would learn something else that would make me older still. But I went in anyway, for no other reason than it was the next place to go.

The wood floor creaked and my mother's head jerked in my direction. When she saw me, she began sobbing. Now I know that the tears were not so much about her own sorrow as they were about her fear of what the news would mean to me. That fear made it impossible for her to speak, so the neighbor who sat next to her on our blue couch said the words instead.

I never saw her again, my bandit-faced dog, the one who knew how to nuzzle and whimper when I needed her most. The neighbor had witnessed the car that hit Bandit drive away, leaving her dead in the middle of the street. The neighbor had run to our house to waken my mother. I suppose they wanted to protect me, so they had her buried while I was still at school. I don't know for sure, but I think I was in algebra class when she died.

But it was too late for their protection. I had already seen too much on that road in front of our house for anybody to protect me from anything ever again. So when night fell, I took my place on the front porch as usual. And kept watch.

Harley James passed by in his blue pickup, leaning toward the left out of town. This time Mabel sat in the passenger's seat. I saw Harley's right arm strike backwards, hitting her square across the face. I never knew if she cried.

I hugged my knees to my chest to stave off a shiver, a response to what I had just seen, and rocked back enough to look above me. Stars blinked slowly, angel eyes in the heavens, according to my mama. As was my custom, I flung a prayer upwards towards them, this time for Bandit and Mabel. A long breath released with the amen. And then a breeze, like a silent blessing, came carrying the faint scent of lilac.

Realization

by
Marilyn Lorenz

Yesterday merganser ducks that winter on our pond
rose quietly and left for cooler climes.
I walk to the empty pond with a can of corn,
and throw it on the grass, sadly.

The still, cold pond and spring-blue sky,
the new green leaves that meet my eye,
the first brave buds of color in my garden
cannot dispel such loss.

Some mysterious pull of nature
hurried them on their way,
soaring and drifting through a sky
far from my searching eye.

It no longer matters what my intentions were.
I'd sought to feed our children too, long ago,
only to find them gone, quietly,
a day too soon.

Home of the Brave

by
Bobbi Hahn

While waiting to board a flight out of Savannah recently, I noticed a large number of military personnel in the gate area. They were all men accompanied by what I assumed were various family members. One, a strikingly handsome, tall black man was with an older woman and a little girl—his mother and daughter, I imagined. Several sat with wives and young children, sharing those last few minutes together. Some of the wives were wearing t-shirts printed with the message: "My husband is serving over there." Another man stood with an older gentleman who I guessed was his father; they hugged fiercely just before he boarded.

I tried not to invade their privacy, but it was hard not to look at each group as they said their tearful goodbyes. There was just so much raw emotion. They were all dressed in light brown desert fatigues, not the jungle green from other years—so I knew where they were going. Most of them looked *so young* . . . surely much too young to be going off to war, in such a far off place.

My zone was the last to board; as each man passed by, I read the nametag sewn onto the front of his fatigues, whispered a quiet thank you, then said a quick prayer asking God to bless him and keep him safe. By the time the last man boarded, I was barely able to keep from sobbing. I cannot imagine how difficult it was for those guys and their families.

From conversations overheard during the course of the flight, I learned that most of the men were returning from leave. In my opinion, that would have made their leaving again even more difficult. As we began the initial descent into Atlanta, the captain announced, as they often do these days, that several soldiers were aboard; and he just wanted them to know how much we all appreciated their service to our country. Then he added a request that, upon landing, all of us remain seated, allowing the military to deplane first because they had a tight connection.

When we got to our gate, the rest of us stayed in our seats while the soldiers gathered their backpacks and other gear as they waited in the aisle. That is when the plane erupted into spontaneous applause, accompanied by calls of "God Bless," "Be Safe," "Hope you come home soon," and "Bravo, Man!" Of course, my tears began again, and I felt a great surge of pride in my fellow Americans because these brave young men were being sent off with love and blessings from total strangers! The good wishes continued with many pats on their backs as they passed through the plane until finally it was just us. We gathered our belongings, looking at one another with a small smile or a brief nod, and went off to business meetings, reunions with family, or a continuation of our journeys. While those strong, precious young men—U.S. soldiers—went off to war, making our peaceful everydayness possible.

Godspeed . . .

Homemade Fig Preserves

by
Frederick W. Bassett

Back in Alabama, I stop to see Elsie Brewer.
Knocking on the farmhouse door,
I'm thinking, She may be the next to go.
The door's unlocked . . . Come on in . . .
Lord a'mercy, it's you, Fred.
I been perished to death to see you.
Twisted and curled, her hands look helpless
like the legs that won't give her two steps.
But I see the calloused hands of a girl
who had to plow like a man or else
her drunkard father, plow rope doubled
and doubled again, would beat her to the ground.
You might think I get lonesome out here,
but they ain't but a few folks I care to see.
And there's that one cousin who helps me out.
She taught me how to be a weaver. Lord,
I'm glad you never had to work in no cotton mill.
Those old textile hands are folded in her lap
as she huddles in the wheelchair.
But I see the kind hands of a young woman
who longed to care for the sick,
not knowing that nurses don't nurse
from a correspondence course
advertised in a dime store magazine.
Fred, I've got a little something for you
before you go. I had a hard time finding figs
this year. But what I got turned out good.
Leaving, I'm thinking, These will be the last
preserves I'll ever get from her.
Do I eat them or store them like memories?
My dear old women are dying too fast.

Hands

by
Art Cornell

These old hands
Have felt and done so much,
So much.
When young
They were always ready,
Clenched and proud.
They held life
And even death
And more precious still—
Love.
Now in age
My faithful companions
Have more lines
And folds,
More softness,
Less anger.
They have done so much
For me on our journey together,
And still
They perform,
Sometimes with difficulty,
To touch,
To hold,
To offer prayers.
These old hands.

Henry's Diet

by

Jim Van Cleave

Henry Bosworth pulled his 2008 Corvette into the parking place in front of the Doctors' Pavilion near the Hilton Head Regional Medical Center. He sat in the driver's seat for a moment and took a deep breath.

It's just my annual physical, he thought, *absolutely nothing to worry about*. Still, he had a shadow of a doubt. He was nearly fifty and under a lot of stress. His father had his first heart attack at about his age. He wondered for the thousandth time if it ran in the family. Then there was his weight. He knew he was at least twenty-five pounds too heavy, and the doctor would rag him about it. He did it every year.

No stranger to self-deception, Henry took off his watch, a bulky sports model. From his wallet he extracted a few bills for his co-pay and deposited his watch and wallet in the center console. *No point in weighing anything I don't have to*, he thought. He labored out of the low-slung car, chirped the door lock, and slipped the keys into his jacket pocket.

He hung up his coat along with the four ounces of keys and signed in at the reception desk for Dr. Grant. "The doctor will be with you in a few minutes," a chunky receptionist announced. "Just have a seat."

I wonder if Grant gives her grief about her weight, too, he mused.

He occupied himself by studying the other patients in the waiting room. A woman was sitting behind her walker. A man with a portable oxygen machine waited with his wife, who was solicitously patting his arm. A seventy-something man entered on crutches, followed by an attractive woman Henry judged to be in her early forties. She helped the gimpy man sit and then signed him in. *His daughter*, Henry mentally speculated. *At least there's one other healthy person here.*

Fifteen minutes passed, and Henry started to get agitated. *The office opens at nine and I was here at five to. What are they doing back there? He's probably chatting up the nurses and having a cup of coffee while I sit here getting depressed looking at all these sick people.*

Ten minutes later Henry was paging through an ancient copy of *Modern Maturity* when a hawk-faced nurse popped her head through the door to the inner sanctum and called his name. "Mr. Bosworth, the doctor will see you now."

He tore himself away from an article on retirement communities which pictured incredibly fit seventy-year-olds playing tennis and square dancing. As he followed Nurse Ratched through the door, he pictured her in leather bondage gear flogging a helpless patient who had the temerity to ask for Viagra.

"Before you see the doctor, we need to check your weight. Step up on the scales, please."

Here it comes, he thought, quickly shedding his shoes. *I just dumped another eight ounces.*

"That really isn't necessary. We subtract five pounds for clothes."

"Well, I had on kind of heavy shoes," he lied. He had deliberately selected his Italian loafers with wafer-thin soles.

The nurse set the balance weight at 150 and edged the slide past the 190 mark. At 199.5 the bar still would not rise off the peg. Henry broke into a cold sweat as she moved the balance to 200. The final result was 202. Without comment she recorded the result. "You can wait in here." She gestured to the first room on her right. "I'll take your blood pressure, and then Dr. Grant will see you."

She told him to sit on the examining table and velcroed the pressure cuff to his arm. "Relax now. This won't hurt a bit." She pumped vigorously and then slowly released the pressure. "Not bad, Mr. Bosworth . . . 130 over 75. You probably won't have a stroke today," she said gaily. "Strip down to your shorts, and the doctor will be in soon."

Henry sat miserably on the paper covering of the examination table, which stuck to his sweaty thighs and quickly became wrinkled as he nervously shifted his weight. For another ten minutes he studied anatomical charts of healthy hearts and livers hung on the wall. He wondered if his organs looked as pink and healthy as the ideals depicted. *Probably not*, he decided.

He was about to convince himself he was having mild chest pains when Dr. Grant burst though the door, his laptop under his arm. "Henry, it's good to see you again!" He grasped Henry's hand and shook it heartily.

"Nice to be here, Dr. Grant," he fibbed, feeling incredibly self-conscious in his plaid boxers with his belly hanging over the waistband.

"Call me Jim, please. How's your golf game? You're a member at Sea Pines, right."

When did doctors get so young? This guy wasn't a day over thirty-five. "I'm in a little slump, but I can still break ninety." Grant appeared not to be paying attention to his answer. Instead, he was vigorously typing on his laptop, apparently recording his weight and blood pressure.

"That's good," Dr. Jim replied not looking up. "My wife and I are social members, but I don't have time for golf . . . young kids you know."

Actually, Henry didn't know. When his kids were young, he still managed to play at least twice a week—on Saturdays with the guys and on Sundays with his wife. But that was back when it was still okay to leave your young kids with a neighborhood teenager and have some time to yourself. It was also before Blackberries and iPhones and the whole 24/7 work nonsense. Henry was caught up in that now himself. Ten years ago, after his wife left him, he'd quit his job as a CPA in Cleveland, moved to Hilton Head, and gotten his real estate license. For a long time it had been smooth sailing. Property values rose, and so did his income. Then real estate prices tanked, credit dried up; and now he was hustling just to keep up the payments on his Corvette and condo, to say nothing of his son's college tuition bills. His girlfriend, Nancy, was another expense, but worth it.

"Let's listen to that heart," Grant said, putting aside his computer. A few deep breaths later he announced: "Sounds good. Let's go over the results of your blood work." The doctor handed Henry a sheet of paper with columns of indecipherable numbers on it. "Let's see; cholesterol's a little high at 201; but your HDLs good, so nothing to worry about. Triglycerides are normal, and your PSA is low. That's good."

Henry had only a dim idea about what he was talking about. "So I'm in good shape," he ventured.

"As far as the tests go. As long as you stay on your blood pressure and cholesterol medicines, you should be fine; but there *is* a problem."

Uh oh, he thought.

"Henry, your weight is out of control. You've gained five pounds since your last checkup. You are officially borderline *obese!*"

Henry groaned inwardly. He knew he was a bit overweight, but *obese* did not describe it. He tried to make light of the situation. "Gosh, Doc, I've only gained a pound a year for twenty-five years."

Grant was not amused. "That may be so, but you've picked up five in the last twelve months. Ideally, you should weigh 175 to 180." In a more sympathetic tone he went on. "Henry, I lost thirty pounds a few years ago. It was easy. Look at this."

He swiveled in his chair, reached for a shelf behind him, and thrust a framed picture of himself at Henry. The photo showed a much heavier Dr. Grant with his arm around a small boy, presumably his son. The doctor was smiling gamely at the camera with a roll of fat stretching his polo shirt unattractively.

Henry glanced furtively at his own spare tire. "Wow, that's some transformation. How did you do it?"

"I'll tell you, but first let me ask you a question."

"Sure."

"How many drinks do you have a day?"

"Well, I have a couple before dinner every night." This was a lie. The honest answer was at least four. He needed them to wind down from a day of dealing with window-shopping home buyers with grandiose ideas and no credit.

"Okay, how about after dinner?"

"I never drink after dinner." Another lie. How could he get to sleep without a Scotch or two?

Grant cocked his head at him skeptically. "Look, Henry, a drink or two a day won't hurt you. But don't kid yourself; there's one hundred calories in every ounce of booze. You do the math. Let's just say you average five drinks a day. That's thirty-five hundred calories a week! If you cut those out, you'd lose nearly a pound a week."

Henry was under the impression that vodka had almost no calories and said so. "Doc, vodka is eighty percent water. It can't be fattening."

Grant chuckled knowingly. "That's a popular misconception, but it's not true."

Henry mentally totaled up his daily intake and decided he was closer to four thousand calories a week than the thirty-five hundred Grant had postulated. "Okay, how did you lose all that weight?"

"I stopped drinking altogether for ten weeks, and I lost fifteen pounds. It just melted off." He patted his flat midriff smugly. Since then I only have a drink or two on social occasions, and I've kept on losing."

Henry wondered if he would start again when he could pass for an Auschwitz survivor.

As if reading his thoughts Grant said, "When your body finds its natural weight, you'll stabilize. Do you think you could try my system?"

Henry said dubiously, "I'd sure miss those before-dinner cocktails."

"I'm sure you would, for a time. But if you can't get along without them, that's another problem altogether," he said ominously. "Now drop your shorts and roll over on your right side. Let's see how that prostate is doing."

That evening Henry was telling Nancy about the doctor's visit and enjoying his third vodka and tonic—made with diet tonic, of course.

"My vital signs are okay, but he got on me about my weight. He always does. He's lost a lot of weight, and he wants me to do the same. There's nothing more insufferable than someone who has kicked a bad habit and wants to tell you about it."

"What was his bad habit?" Nancy's legs were tucked under her on the couch across from him, and she looked terrific in bare feet, black slacks, and a red sweater.

"Apparently he gained a lot of weight because of his drinking. So he cut it out for a while and now drinks only at parties. He showed me a picture of him when he was fat, and there's no denying he looks a lot better now."

"Well, Henry, what do you think? He could be on to something. You are a little heavy."

"Please, Nancy, don't you start on me. I love it when we get together in the evening, have a few drinks, and unwind from the day. Your job at the *Packet* involves a lot of stress, too. That glass of wine you're sipping is doing the same thing for you that my vodka tonics do, right?"

"Sure, but I have one glass, two at the most. You have three or four. There's a difference between unwinding and getting unwound."

"Are you saying I'm a drunk?" Henry was getting angry.

"Calm down, sweetie. No, you're not a lush. But you do drink too much for your own good. I worry that when you leave here, Sea Pines security might stop you; and you couldn't pass a Breathalyzer. Did you ever think about that?"

Henry stared mournfully into his empty glass and jiggled the ice cubes. "I was just telling you what the doctor said. Besides, I drive very carefully."

"And you think driving twenty-five in a thirty-five zone won't attract attention?"

"They'll just think I'm a tourist," Henry offered weakly. "Let's go get some dinner . . . how about the Sage Room?"

"Let's just order pizza and see what happens afterwards," Nancy countered with a wink.

On the way back to his condo Henry kept the Corvette at a steady thirty-five down South Sea Pines Drive. He mentally tallied up the evening's drinks. *Four vodkas and two glasses of wine with dinner. If Grant's right, that's six hundred calories on top of three slices of Guiseppe's Special. If I have a single malt before bed, I'm up to seven hundred in booze alone!* Then a terrible thought hit him as he turned into his parking space. *What if those drinks weren't one ounce but two?* Which he had to admit they probably were. *God, I'm over a thousand on the calorie meter.*

As he settled in to watch David Letterman, swirling a snifter of Glenmorangie, he solemnly vowed to think about all of this in the morning.

Morning came and with it a slight headache, which Henry attributed to the single malt. *Maybe I should cut back some,* he thought. *I'll see if I can get through the evening without a drink before dinner,* he promised himself. *How hard can it be?*

The day passed quietly enough with two showings, no sales, and dozens of games of computer solitaire. At five he closed up the office and went home to shower and put on some comfortable clothes. He was about to reach for the vodka bottle to make himself the first drink of the evening when he remembered his early morning promise to himself. He resisted the temptation and felt good about it. After his shower he put on a golf shirt and a pair of freshly ironed khakis. The waist band was uncomfortably tight, and he had to suck in his gut to button them. *That's it. I've got to do something!*

On the five-minute drive to Nancy's place he felt strange, sort of disconnected. He was out of his routine and facing an uncertain future. It reminded him of how he felt when he had quit smoking years ago. For days after he quit, everything reminded him of cigarettes—the first cup of coffee in the morning, staring glumly at the ash tray on the table beside the newspaper; the stale-smoke smell of his car's upholstery on his drive to work; the blue haze in the conference room as his coworkers maddeningly puffed away. But he had gotten through that and was proud of having kicked his two-pack-a-day habit. Wasn't quitting drinking the same thing? Somehow he did not think so. Almost nobody smoked these days, but everybody he knew drank. And what about after golf? He thought about the taste of an ice cold Sam Adams after a round and nearly swerved off the road.

Stop it, he chided himself. *Let's think positively here. We're talking about quitting to lose weight, not quitting forever. Hadn't Dr. Jim said he still had a few drinks on social occasions?* This made Henry feel better, and he made it to Nancy's without further incident.

She greeted him at the door with a warm kiss and led him into the living room. "Make yourself a drink," she said, "And then join me on the couch. I have some good news."

Henry went to the small bar and hesitated. *This is it*, he thought. He stared at the bottle of Absolut for a long moment and then filled his glass with ice cubes and diet tonic. He took a tentative sip. *Almost like the real thing*, he decided. Returning to the living room, he sat on the couch and said, "So what's your news, sweetheart?"

"Oh, Henry, I'm so excited. They promoted me to assistant editor with a nice raise. I'm in charge of the editorial page three days a week, and I'm expected to write features for the Lowcountry section. No more chasing around Bluffton trying to get stories about bicycle thefts and domestic violence complaints."

"Nancy, that's wonderful! I couldn't be happier for you." He meant it and leaned over to give her a congratulatory kiss. "We should go out and celebrate."

"No, Henry. I planned for us to stay in tonight, just the two of us. I made a pasta primavera, and we can open a bottle of champagne."

"That sounds absolutely wonderful, but I don't know about the champagne."

"What are you talking about? You love champagne, and this is a special occasion."

"I'm on the wagon. I guess they still call it that."

"You mean you're not drinking? What's that in your hand?"

"It's just tonic, hon. I'm trying to take Dr. Grant's advice." Henry felt terrible. He did not want to disappoint her and ruin the celebration.

Apparently she was not upset because she said, "That's wonderful. I'm proud of you." With that she threw her arms around him and gave him a delicious kiss.

"Wow, if I'd known I'd get this reaction, I would have quit long ago."

"I can't wait to see you skinny!"

"Don't hold your breath. This could take a while."

The rest of the evening was wonderful—the dinner and the lovemaking. Aside from stifling a few burps brought on by four glasses of fizzy tonic water, it was perfect. Henry even thought his performance in bed was improved by virtue of being totally aware of what he was doing for the first time in a long time.

It was almost midnight when they kissed at Nancy's front door. Henry hummed to himself as he walked to his car enjoying the warm spring night with the scent of jasmine in the air.

He turned right and headed down South Sea Pines Drive toward his condo two miles away, aware that, for the first time in ages, he didn't have to be worried if he was pulled over.

He had gone only about a mile when a car with no lights barreled through the stop sign at South Beach Lane and plowed into his front fender, spinning the Corvette 180 degrees. For a moment Henry sat stunned in his seat, batting feebly at the deflated air bag in his lap. When he realized he was not seriously injured, he opened his door and got out of the car to see if anyone in the other car was hurt. He reached the passenger's side door of what he saw was a 5 Series BMW with a severely collapsed front end.

Henry pounded on the window and saw there was no one in the right-hand seat. However, he could see the driver on the other side slumped over the wheel. He sprinted around the car, in what passed for a sprint for Henry, and jerked open the door.

"Hey, buddy, are you all right? Should I call a doctor?"

The passenger looked up at him blearily and said in a shaky voice, "I *am* a doctor."

Suddenly he recognized the man, and at the same time got a strong whiff of alcohol. "Jesus, Dr. Grant. It's you! Have you been drinking?"

"Oh, hi. Henry-something, isn't it?" The doctor waved a hand in Henry's general direction. "Sorry about this. It's my poker night," as if this answered Henry's question.

"See if you can get out of the car. Let me help you."

"No, no. I'm okay. I can get out on my own."

Grant struggled out of his seat belt and stood unsteadily in the street. A siren sounded in the distance.

At a loss for words, Henry blurted, "I thought you didn't drink."

With one eye closed as if to prevent there from being two Henrys, the doctor said, "Only on social occasions."

Seasons Change
by Art Cornell

God set the sky
On slow simmer,
Roiling the clouds
Into black and gray
Masses of air
Touching the tree tops
With angst.

Storm
by Art Cornell

The wind, now calm,
Was like a child
Scolded,
Almost meek,
Yet
Ready to
Throw a tantrum
At the twist of a cloud.

The Old Enmity

by
Frederick W. Bassett

My father passed it on to me with good cause,
knowing how I would ramble
the day away in the old fields and forests
of the fallow farm. At six, I followed
him down the cow trail that cut
through the woods to the swimming hole,
unaware of that wondrous surge
for fight or flight before he went mad,
throwing rock after rock
until the snake's head was mush.
"Rattlesnake pilot," he said,
using the local name for the copperhead.
Rage draining away, he was telling me
about the venomous fangs of the old foe,
when his eye caught the second copperhead,
coiled just above my heels, its broad head
pointing like a drawn arrow, tongue
flicking for the center of my heat.
After that fight, voice trembling, he said,
"Son, you got to watch out for snakes.
Run as fast as you can when you see one."
At ten, I'd had enough of flight
when I saw the little green devil
sunning on the garden wire fence.
I loaded Dad's twelve-gauge shotgun,
cocked the hammer, and blasted its head off.

As an older boy, I once offered my heel
to a rattlesnake. Saw it just in time
to jump back out of reach.
A second look turned it into a stick.
Years later, I would tell that story
to my philosophy students and ask,
"Did I see a snake or a stick?"
"A stick," someone typically answered.
"Oh, but I saw a rattlesnake, saw the copper
diamonds on its back, never been more certain
about what I saw." Then somebody
would say, "So you saw a snake."
"No! No! I saw a stick.
Picked it up, laughing my head off."
True, I laughed at myself for hatching
a snake from a stick. Still I kept
my father's sharp eye for the old enemy
that day and soon found its paper-thin skin.
I've never seen a snake shed its old skin.
But I've sloughed off a thing or two
to make room for others, even poisonous ones.
So when the dean's wife called in near hysterics,
I rushed over to make peace.
"It's just a rat snake. Big but harmless.
I'll drag it down in the woods."
"No, kill it. Please, you've got to kill it."
You can forget reason.
That old enmity strikes deep.

The Gifts of an Addict Daughter

by
Marilyn Lorenz

I kept each one
because they mark your sorrow,
and my helplessness,
in ways that failed words.
Like translucent skin
covering our bond's bones,
they hid a starving child
in expected wrappings.
Paid for with brokenness,
offered in unfelt hope,
they shame me across time,
burning my hands as I lift them,
one by one.

Midnight Requisitioning

by
James Edward Alexander

Every noncommissioned officer in the armed forces develops the ability to . . . steal. Regardless of the quantity of resources allocated for a military mission, it is almost guaranteed that the supply will be exhausted before the assignment is completed. Noncommissioned officers (NCOs) have, therefore, devised a military-wide system for obtaining needed supplies outside the supply channels. It is called "midnight requisitioning," a nice euphemism for . . . stealing; sort of like robbing Peter to pay Paul. Almost any service member understands the rules for temporarily borrowing from another source what is needed to get the job done.

While serving as a ward master at Lackland Air Force Base hospital in the 1950s, my requisitioning skills were honed with the help of three subordinates. Each month all ward masters were required to account for their allotted linen inventory of towels, wash cloths, pillow cases, and sheets. Each month my count was short until I figured out the cause.

If we took to the linen exchange 120 dirty sheets, 60 bath towels, 40 hand towels, and 20 washcloths, the supply sergeant issued clean replacements in tied bundles, each bundle supposedly containing ten items. Sometimes the bundles contained only eight or nine items. There was no time to count each bundle before leaving the supply warehouse, and arguing with the supply sergeant was worse than accepting the deficits. Over the period of a month these nickel and dime shortages could be significant. My subordinates told me they would handle the problem in a manner that would leave me blameless if their efforts were detected. I cautioned them to "do the right thing."

This was their plan: Some time between 0100 and 0200 hours, one of them strolled down the ramp to another ward and engaged that night corpsman in conversation and a smoke outside the front door. Simultaneously, the second errant guy entered the back door and went straight to the linen closet and improved our inventory. They were so efficient as to need a gurney to transport their booty, which the third man wheeled along the road behind the wards.

The next week I got calls from other ward masters who inquired if I had any surplus linen and offered me various favors in exchange for a few sheets, hand towels, and pillow cases.

After almost a year my troops voluntarily disclosed their technique. Until then, I did not ask; they did not tell.

Not many years later I was in charge of a team of GIs as we traveled on special assignments throughout Europe. One night we flew from Scotland to a base in Germany aboard a slow moving but reliable C-47, nicknamed the "Gooney Bird." We arrived around 0200 hours, tired, hungry, and after the dining hall had closed. Our quarters were in a house used by military families that was temporarily vacant. There were ample cooking utensils; but we needed something to cook, so we went searching for food. Our target was the hospital where there is always something to eat; and as a former ward master, I knew where to find it. En route we spotted the truck that supplied food to all of the dining halls. Two persons were assigned to distract the driver while the rest of us entered the well-stocked vehicle to "requisition" eggs, bacon, milk, sausage, butter, coffee, sugar, salt, and pepper. Just as we exited what had become our impromptu commissary, a car approached. The high beam headlights illuminated our operation. The driver was a brigadier general who had just piloted a plane from England and was also looking for food. This commander knew precisely what we were doing.

He asked, "Sergeant, do you know where a man might get something to eat at this time of day?"

My straightforward answer was, "Well, sir, we're taking care of that right now; and you're welcome to have breakfast with us."

Just then somebody remembered that we had forgotten to get bread. The general offered, "Let me get it."

After he exited the truck with enough bread to feed the multitude, he followed us home for breakfast and a card game of hearts, explaining, "If I'm going to enjoy the fruits of this 'midnight requisition,' I might as well participate."

A Lid Slipped down over the Eye

by
Sharon Rice

I cross the street
and step toward your red brick house,
redder in February's early morning sunlight.

The porch swing stirs.
From what, I wonder?
A breeze promising spring?
Or energy left behind by the shadow
of those who have just risen and gone inside?

The swing where we pushed
our bare summer feet, slow,
against the gray pavement
and rocked while we held hands,
as soft toward each other as the falling rain.

And dreamed . . .
of great white houses with porches on three sides
and rooms where we would go to do our
            separate work
filled with light from tall windows.

I climb the steps and place my letter to you
in the brass mailbox
and remember days I carried what was there
to lay on your oak kitchen table,
waiting for your return from some city.

Today your door—still decorated
with Christmas wreath and red bow—is shut.
And the white slatted blinds
I used to open to the morning,
lie closed—
like a lid slipped down over the eye.

Autumn Fading

by
Robert Hamel

His breath hastens the falling
of red leaves as he watches
the placid earth
awaken from a night of deep slumber.

What will today bring?
Only he knows of yesterdays
and what tomorrow will
uncover from the black veil.

The reds drift with
yellows, oranges, golds
and browns,
as the stream cleanses them all.

Today's greens will morph
to become vivid colors
like the Monarch
hatching from its chrysalis.

Finally, browns lie down
into the dust
awaiting rebirth
in purity and joy.

The reward of humility

A True Confederate

by
Greg Smorol

The force of the blow knocked me down, leaving me dazed and motionless. I was bleeding heavily from the hole left in my chest by the musket ball. Lying still on the ground, I must have looked like I was dead already. When the Yanks ran past our position on the hill, they did not have the time to take prisoners, so they ran a bayonet through anyone who looked alive. They took one look at me and just ran past, not even bothering to use the bayonet. They either thought I was dead, or they just left me to die.

I regained some strength after the Yanks had finished their carnage and had left the hilltop to join the battle below. The smoke from the black powder of the muskets and cannon still hung close to the ground and blocked most of my vision. With the exception of some nearby fallen soldiers and other destruction, I could see little. As near as I could determine, all of my men were dead or dying; and the Yanks had won the skirmish. I propped myself up and vowed that I would not die like this. I always thought that I had been put on this earth for a purpose; and until that purpose was served, I needed to carry on.

I opened my shirt and looked at the hole that was still oozing blood from my chest. The blood was not spurting, so I knew the bullet had not hit an artery. That meant that I might survive if I could just hang on for the medics to arrive. By tearing off a section of cloth from my undershirt and wadding it up, I was able to plug the wound. When my fingers forced the cloth into the bullet hole, I almost fainted from the pain. I lay still for a spell until the blood stopped draining from my system. My patch had worked, and my chances for survival had increased. I pulled myself over to the line of cannon still facing down the hill and found a spot that looked down into the valley. I could only watch and wait for help to arrive.

While I lay there resting, my mind shifted to the days before when I was given command of the hill. I had been put in charge of the group of men who were to protect the rear flank of the Confederate Army in the valley below.

The general told me, "Sam, we must stop the Union Army that has been descending from the North laying waste to the land and killing everyone in sight. We have had small skirmishes with them, but I am looking for a more advantageous position for the fight yet to come. Our troops are digging in where the valley narrows and has steep cliffs to protect our army's sides, allowing only a frontal assault. Our rear is protected by the miles of deep valley leading into the heart of the South. However, on one side, behind the army, there is a small rounded hill that forms a pass that could provide access to our rear. Because of this, I am fortifying the hill with five cannon and a goodly amount of men. Your job is to command those men and hold back the Yanks. If anything goes wrong, send a messenger."

I remembered when I first saw the narrow pass over the hill, I had thought it would not be wise to attack it. It would be a death trap for anyone trying to do so.

However, I learned war is not always made up of wise decisions. I was confronted by a large contingent of Yanks that had been dispatched to pass over that hill and get behind the enemy lines. When they first arrived, they charged up the hill only to be greeted by our heavy cannon fire and a deadly barrage of musket fire. I did not know that the leader of the Union troops felt he must succeed, whatever the cost, if his army was to be victorious in the larger battle in the valley below. In desperation, he had directed hourly charges that had wiped out many of my troops, as well as many of his own soldiers.

I thought of how the Yanks had set up sniper fire that cut down a number of my men. However, I knew I still had five cannon that were devastating the Union troops and stopping them from joining up with the rest of the Union Army.

I visualized the last ditch effort, when the Yanks had charged up the hill like madmen. They had let the cannon take their toll but charged on before the cannon could be reloaded. The carnage at the top of the hill was unholy. Bodies lay everywhere, and no man was spared or captured. The Yanks were not taking prisoners, and the vastly outnumbered Rebels were determined to fight to the last man. The quickness of the surprise turnaround in the battle for the hill left me no time to think about warning the army below.

I knew if the hill were captured, the Yanks would be able to sneak down into the valley to join up with the rest of their army. We had held the hill for two days. I felt we were in control and could hold our position. I had not been prepared for the massive onslaught that occurred. Now my men lay dead; there was no one left to send as a messenger to the general.

My mind returned to my current condition. A slight breeze started to pass over the hill and thinned some of the smoke hanging around like a dense morning fog. I squinted and saw the battle lines forming in the valley below. The armies seemed fairly even in number, and I could see our army had the better position.

I watched as the Northerners spread out to form a line in front of the Confederates. They gathered in the middle and charged the Rebel line, but it held firm. I saw the Yanks charge a few more times, but they were losing a lot of men and were not gaining any ground. I was feeling good about seeing the defeat of the Yanks, until I saw the

Union troops descending from our own hill towards the rear of the Rebel forces.

I knew that it had been my responsibility to stop those men and protect the army below. My men and I had fought valiantly but had failed. Now the Confederate Army below was in jeopardy. All of my men had been killed. There was no one to warn the army below of the approaching danger.

I tried to move. The pain was excruciating, and the blood again began to seep from my wound. I thought of my wife and three children and knew I must remain still if I were to see them ever again. I dozed off, more weakened from the loss of blood than weariness. I slept fitfully. My mind drifted to my small five-acre farm. I dreamed about my wife, brave and supportive as I was chosen for duty.

I could hear her words as she said, "Sam, this is not a war that we wanted, but it is one that we have to fight. We need to protect our farm and provide a safe place where our children can grow up. Be careful, and always remember that we are waiting here for you no matter what."

I saw my two young daughters, their long hair flowing behind them, tears in their eyes, as they watched me march off to war. But it was the image of my small son, standing in his baggy, well-patched farm trousers that struck the cord that aroused me from my slumber. My son's large brown eyes had also been filled with tears, but his tears had been caused by his immense pride for his father—a pride that I knew must never be sullied.

When I awoke, I saw the Union troops—the ones that had overtaken our hill—preparing for a charge against the rear of the main Rebel army. They were hidden in a hollow behind the Rebel lines, and it looked like they were trying to coordinate their attack with the next Union charge from the front. I could see there would be a total rout of the Rebel army, and the death toll would be horrendous.

It was this thought that caused a light to flicker in my soul. I felt I needed to remain still to survive and return to my family. But I also knew if I did not try to warn the army below, I would never be able to look my son in the eye again. No one would ever know what happened, but my own shame would be too much to bear. I had rested and now had some strength left within my body. I was determined to use that strength as best I could. Sure, I had my family to think of; but so did every man in the army below.

I was very weak and could not stand up without help. I looked around and grabbed a rifle to help me get to my feet. I hobbled over to the cannon to my left. My men had partially reloaded the cannon before they were killed. I lifted a cannon shell into the barrel and finished the reloading process. The weight of the shell caused my chest to heave and the bleeding to start again. I rotated the cannon towards the hollow below and lined up the trajectory as best I could. I was out of breath and fatigued. I needed to pause and regain some strength before I could finish reloading and aligning the next cannon.

Thoughts of the impending disaster for the army below and the welfare of my family caused courage to flow within my veins. I continued on—gasping, cramping, crawling, stumbling, bleeding, and painfully reloading and aligning the other cannon. I looked for a fire to touch them off. There was only smoke that was dying off too.

I fell to the ground and cried for help. I asked God for the strength to finish the job I had started out to do. There was only silence as I lay on my back dying from the effort I had expended to load the cannons. My head rolled to one side. My eyes glazed over, and I felt a peace coming on that I had not felt before.

I flicked my eyelids, but it seemed my sight was still a bit fuzzy. I strained to clear my vision and saw that the fuzz was a piece of wick that was used to fire the cannons. It was lying near my face, right by my eyes. My heart grew strong, and I used all of the strength left within me to gather up the wick and move it over by a smoldering log. I blew on the wick and the log until a flame appeared. I staggered over to the first cannon, using a ramrod to help me stand up. I positioned myself in a line with the next cannon, lit the fuse, and began to hobble away, still using the ramrod as a crutch. As I lit the next fuse, the first cannon exploded, firing its round towards the hollow. I continued on in this manner until I reached the last cannon and lit that fuse. I fell over the cannon as it fired its round.

The shock from the cannon blast ripped apart my wounds, and I knew it would end my life. That did not matter to me anymore. I had found the superhuman strength within myself that had allowed me to complete this mission, and protect my son's pride.

I could see that the Union troops hidden in the hollow were about to charge when the first round flew over their head and landed between them and the rebels. The explosion served to alert the Rebels to the danger behind them.

The Rebel general, situated at the rear of the Confederate lines, knew the hilltop pass had been breached. He immediately started yelling commands.

"The Yanks have gotten over the pass and are behind us. Start setting up a defensive line in front of that hollow."

At first the general had feared the worst. He presumed they were caught between two lines with no way to escape. As they began setting up their defenses for an attack from the rear, the general was trying to figure out how to cut his losses to a minimum.

The next two rounds landed squarely within the hollow and routed the Union soldiers. Their numbers had been greatly reduced by the battle on the hilltop, and the cannon fire killed scores of men who had been bunched together preparing to attack.

There was panic, causing the Union soldiers to run in all directions in disarray, giving away their position and the element of surprise. The fourth round caught them in the flank and built upon the panic rampant within their ranks. It was the fifth and final round that sealed their fate. The last thing I saw through glazed and burning eyes was the round falling short of the hollow but making a direct hit on the command post.

Epilogue

The Union commanders were killed, and their troops were left to fend for themselves. This created even greater chaos within the Union troops. The Confederate general used the pandemonium to seize the advantage. He shouted out to his captains: "Set up a three-pronged attack on the Union forces behind us. Send out several score of men to circle around each side of the hollow and set up a line to fire from. Then send the main force of our attack right up the center of the hollow."

The Union soldiers, now without leadership, fought off the main thrust of the attack for a short time and then scrambled to the left and right trying to escape. Most men ran up over the sides of the hollow, fully exposed to the Confederate lines waiting for them. They were cut down like cattle in a pen. A few turned and ran back into the hollow, only to fall victim to the main force waiting for them. Not one Union soldier escaped the trap. The Confederate Army's rear flank was safe once again, and they could concentrate on the frontal attacks from the Union forces. They had chosen their spot well, and as the battle progressed, the Union forces were weakened and retreated back up the valley.

The Confederate Army won that day, not because of luck, but because of the dedication of Sam, a true Confederate. Sam was never recognized for his heroics, nor were many of the other brave men who fought that grisly war. However, they were proud men who fought for their beliefs and their families, and their pride will live on forever—the type of pride that Sam had seen burning so brightly in the eyes and heart of his young son—a pride that had never been sullied.

Prayer for My Grandson

by
Marilyn Lorenz

God lift this child from circumstance,
Teach him to speak, to run, to dance,
Help him to add just two and two,
And recognize the color blue.

Sing to him softly in the night,
When he's frightened, hold him tight,
Feed him, clothe him, keep him warm,
Through every terror, every storm.

God, see this boy so far away,
Would you bless him on this day,
With joy and laughter in his play,
His mother's smile, light on his way?

He cannot speak, but locked inside
Are all the thoughts a boy can hide,
That you must know, for you know all,
Thoughts beautiful, thoughts big and small.

This is the prayer I ask of you.
I ask for him, believe anew,
Your power his shield and shelter be,
To lean against mere destiny.

Cottageville

by
Tom Crawford

Horror stories of speed traps, confiscatory fines, redneck law enforcement, and good ol' boy justice have haunted Yankee drivers venturing into the Deep South for decades.

But this driver from the Bay State of Massachusetts had to conclude, after criss-crossing the Palmetto State of South Carolina for more than a decade, that these stories were perhaps exaggerated, if not downright slanderous.

For several winters spent on Hilton Head Island, I scheduled April golf junkets at Myrtle Beach on my trip back north to my residence in Massachusetts. A couple of dozen golfers from the Blackstone Valley of Massachusetts and Rhode Island had been traveling to Myrtle Beach for two decades, and I had been invited to join them from my home golf club at Blissful Meadows in Uxbridge, Massachusetts.

It is nearly a four-hour hop from the southernmost Lowcountry vacationland of Hilton Head Island near Savannah, Georgia, to North Myrtle Beach near the North Carolina line. After permanently settling on Hilton Head, I decided to go cross-country on SC 17A to join my fellow players coming south to Myrtle Beach for the April outing.

By taking this route, I would avoid heavy traffic around Charleston and busy Interstate 95 to the west.

Everything went swimmingly until I hit Cottageville. That is when the cruiser with the flashing lights popped into my rear view mirrors, forcing me to respectfully and dutifully pull over.

"Where are you from?" the officer asked courteously, having already ascertained that my home address was Hilton Head. "Originally?" he said, clarifying his query.

I hedged. "Well," I replied. "I was born in the Blackstone Valley, in Whitinsville, in central Massachusetts, but I have lived much of my adult life in western Massachusetts."

"Where in western Massachusetts?" he persisted.

"Well, I first moved to Springfield but ended up in Wilbraham," I answered.

"I'm from Wilbraham," the officer responded with surprise.

I looked at his nameplate. It said Fernandes. Most Bay Staters recognize the difference between Fernandes and Fernandez, and know that the former are descendants of the Portuguese fishermen who first settled in New Bedford. Many of their countrymen heeded the advice of Horace Greeley to "Go West, young man," and they ended up working in a jute mill in Ludlow, another Springfield suburb. Thus, they spread into the Springfield section of Indian Orchard and the neighboring suburb of Wilbraham.

"Did you have any relatives who played Little League baseball?" I asked.

The answer was in the affirmative, and it turned out his nephews were teammates of my son a few years before.

Officer Fernandes explained that he had been on the Cottageville police force for four years. After a few more pleasant words of conversation and a friendly written warning regarding the 35-mile-per-hour speed limit, we parted amicably.

I subsequently reflected on whether my failure to slow down from 55 to 35 in downtown Cottageville was the only reason I got stopped. South Carolina issues only one rear license plate. I recalled that I had replaced the old Massachusetts one on the front with a vintage Boston Red Sox plate that had been nailed to a stud in my father's basement since the 1940s.

An alert officer Fernandes presumably spotted that plate, felt a little lonely and nostalgic, and decided to enforce the law and satisfy his curiosity simultaneously.

Collector's Red Sox Tag

Photograph by Phyllis Crawford

Driftwood Tree

Photograph by Bobbi Hahn

The Beachcomber

by
Shanti North

Mel sat on her patio bathing in moonlight, transfixed by the bright spell of the full moon and the glowing pathway it cast across the ocean. A warm evening breeze and the quiet lapping of small waves did little to impart the calmness she so desperately needed. This was her last sanctuary, the space that still anchored her spirit to the world. Yet the walls of this last respite were crumbling fast.

Now that Leland was dead, her attachment to life seemed tenuous. She was unable to shake off the depression and grief that cycled through her daily life. Longing to follow her soul mate to that other place, she wondered if the unfathomable distance of moon glow would take her there. Although she feared that event called death, she knew it was a simple thing, a thin veil to push aside and pass through. Where was her courage? She had enough pills to do it. It would be easy just to wash them down with a good vintage wine.

Leland and Melinda Brooks had retired early and moved to Hilton Head Island for the lifestyle, a fitting reward for their years of hard work together. Both craved the excitement and solace of the ocean. They had purchased an older, modest property fronting the beach. Although it was flanked by sprawling mansions, they were satisfied with their seventies-style frame house, a long way from the cold, icy Chicago winters. Retirement pursuits defined their lives: golf, tennis, country club, church, volunteer activism, and summer visits with grandchildren. Life by the sea had been full and rewarding.

It all came to a shocking halt in one split second on that July day. It was hot and sweltering, already in the mid-eighties at 8:00 a.m. Lee had stood on the downstairs patio, dripping in sweat after his morning run on the beach. Mel never saw him die. She was futzing around in the kitchen. When she finally went out to speak to him, he was slumped on the concrete, dead of a heart attack.

Lee had been her closest friend, and his friends had become her friends. In contrast to Mel's shy nature, Lee, with his magnetic personality, had been her anchor and lifeline. Friends had called after his death, but she rarely responded. Now that calls were fewer, oblivion was settling into her life. Each morning that this legacy of grief continued, she struggled to lift her head off her pillow and put her feet on the floor. She was totally and utterly lost without him. What was her next step but to follow his?

She knew her children loved her, but they lived far away and had busy lives. In some way that suited her. They did not need her, and she would not be greatly missed. As if she were already dead, she often felt she lived only in their memory anyway. Now she felt free to go.

On this balmy October night grief refused to budge, and she was desperate for a shift from the pain, one way or another. Perhaps one last walk on the beach would reveal a solution, either to summon the courage to down the pills or, in the heady spell of the full moon, to have a change of heart. Glancing at her reflection in the sliding glass door, she saw a fifty-year-old woman, still shapely and pretty, with a few strands of grey intruding into her dark hair. The sparkling green eyes that had been the signature of her beauty now looked dull and flat. She touched her lips, remembering Lee's kisses. *God, how much I miss him.* She sighed and began walking toward the beach.

She headed in the direction of the Sea Pines beach club. The breeze carried a lovely melody sung by a male voice, accompanied by a guitar. Something in the voice lured her, taking her for a moment away from her misery and the night's purpose.

Maybe the club is still open, though it's kind of late; the music usually ends about ten.

As she got closer, she saw that the club was dark. The music came from near the dune line. She walked closer and saw a man sitting on a gnarly, washed-up tree trunk. Standing still, she listened to his remarkable voice. Normally her reserved nature would have steered her away. She rarely spoke to people on the beach, but that resistance seemed to melt before the notes he sang. Walking closer, she flashed her light to signal her approach. The man looked up and continued to sing; then his lips broadened into a welcoming smile as the song came to an end.

"What a beautiful voice you have. It's extraordinary. Are you someone famous on vacation or a local entertainer? Should I know you?" She caught herself babbling.

"Thanks. I just love to sing. C'mon, I could use an audience." He patted the trunk beside him. "Why don't you sit down? I would be happy to sing for you."

She trusted in that moment and without a word obeyed. As he began to sing again, she studied the handsome figure in front of her. *Younger than I; somewhere under forty.*

In the brightness of the night his skin cast a tanned glow. His eyes were large—dark like polished black granite sparkling in the moonlight. He had strong cheekbones and finely cut features; his full lips now parted in song. Dark hair hung in loose curls down a powerful neck, and his unbuttoned shirt revealed the cut of a muscled chest.

Her mind drifted as the music began to absorb her senses. His beautiful tenor voice ranged through complex melodies. Smooth flowing lyrics spun images of nature: soft, sandy sea shores and far away places. He sang of passion and love. She was caught in a river of music; and a current carried her on a journey that stirred her heart with feelings and visions bound in poetry. Mesmerized in this private concert, she wanted to hear more.

He paused for a moment and looked up at the stars. Preoccupied, he smiled at her but said nothing. Returning his smile, she sat immersed in a musical trance. Looking inward, he played some chords and hummed. After a few minutes he turned to her. "I just got it. Now I have a song meant for your ears only."

She felt a tremble, a warning resounding somewhere deep within her. He sang of loss, longing, and death. The words penetrated, taking her to places shut off and forgotten. Weighty, complicated files of dusty memories emerged. She no longer heard the lyrics as painful recollections drifted to the surface. Images seemed to float by and turned in front of her eyes or in her mind; she was not sure which. *Where is this music taking me, and how could it have such a powerful effect on me?*

Her fingers gripped the sandy old log as if to restrain herself; but too late, a kind of gravity pulled her toward a maelstrom of memories that whirled within.

Lee dead on the patio. *Oh, if only I had known, I could have saved his life, called 911.*

The shuddering pain in her heart as she recalled her father's passing. *So little time with him. I knew he was sick.*

Her mom's death. The miscarriage.

Black, utterly desolate memories flashed like snapshots. Her heart felt as if it would burst with pain. Tears flooded her eyes.

She looked at the stranger spinning his tune. Not missing a beat, he looked back and for a timeless moment locked her into his big, dark eyes. His expression conveyed profound compassion and more. In that moment it seemed there was a transmission of healing as a loving energy streamed through the music, transcending the pain, sending all of the negative feelings and thoughts tumbling out like pieces of gravel.

She saw herself in a vision surrounded in a light brighter than the moon. She felt an unseen touch, an embrace of love that steadied her. In that illuminating moment she became deeply aware that fear, guilt, and loss had robbed her of her self-worth and true identity. She knew she could no longer be defined by negativity. These feelings had twisted her into self-hatred and pushed her to the brink of self-destruction. Now she understood that she was more than all of this. Her life had new pages to be written. Death's signature was gone.

He strummed a final chord, and they sat in silence for a while. Haltingly she asked, "What's happening? I feel like I've been spun 180 degrees in the space of a song."

Gazing out into the moonlit ocean, he replied. "My songs dive deeply into the soul and anchor the truth, a creative illumination, if you will. You're all right, aren't you?" He gave her a steadying look. "Apparently some powerful prayers sent you here tonight. When you walked up, I knew you were in trouble. I could feel the coldness of your heart."

He paused. Then, smiling to lift the mood, he added, "Did you need an attitude adjustment tonight?"

Shaking her head and wiping her tears away, she grinned wryly. "If only you knew. But then it sounds like you did know. You are a strange and mysterious man, indeed. How did you do this to me?"

"The music just assisted you to get from where you were stuck to where you need to be." He tuned his guitar for a moment. "People go out of tune all the time, forgetting what the real music sounds like. I helped you get rid of the discordant noises in your life. And now that you are tuned up, you'll really hear the music and discover that life is a dance."

Mel caught his gaze. "There's magic in your music, and you're more than a singer."

"I am, and I am not," he replied looking away. "You're warmed up now; ready for a smile? Let's pick up the energy and go on a little joy ride beneath the waves. This one's called 'Ocean's Sway.'"

"Do I need to hold on to something?"

He laughed. "Fasten your seat belt." Strumming a G chord, he began the song. She felt light, almost transparent, as if the evening breeze flowed through her and hope shimmered somewhere within. He sang of the ocean; and she felt pulled into it, sensing a salty splash. She looked quickly at her feet but realized they rested on dry sand. Everything around her seemed to be in motion, like the moon on the tide; she felt a strong magnetic pull in the short space between them. She gripped the dead tree trunk to make sure it was not moving. The enchantment deepened as his song took on a visual, holographic quality in the space around her. The words became living images. With a slight gasp, she looked away from them and into his dark eyes.

He gave her a reassuring smile. She reached forward with her mind, diving into the ocean he sang about. A warm, pleasant current swirled around her; she was both inside and outside of the sea. She was swept into the rushing thrill of speeding dolphins diving to great depths; she felt the power and serenity of migrating whales and knew their song. A kaleidoscope of bright, shiny fish swarmed around her—too many to take in. Somewhere in the aqua depths she floated in awe as ghostly jellies drifted in the currents. Flowering reefs undulated brightly in silky rhythms.

When the song ended, she sat bedazzled.

Standing up, he stretched and was silent. Finally he spoke. "You've seen and heard a lot tonight."

"Who are you?" she demanded as she stood up, a little unsteady. "No, don't answer that. I think I know."

He chuckled. "You do? How is that? Okay, let me introduce myself to my beautiful audience of one." He bowed playfully. "My name is Aden. I am just visiting your island; I wanted to explore this beach tonight."

She smiled up at him, realizing he was more than six feet tall. "Do you like it?"

Looking squarely into her eyes, he said, "Right here, right now, I like what I see very much." Mel felt herself flush.

"I'm a beachcomber—nature's troubadour, one might say. I've been traveling the world's beaches forever, it seems. Each place has a vibration, something unique to capture in my music. New places, new songs, new treasures—there is always something new to be discovered. My ear hears what nature wants to say; there are many kinds of minds besides the human mind with thoughts and feelings to be expressed and heard. My music is meant to inspire, transform, and teach pearls of natural wisdom. I find audiences wherever I go—big ones, small ones, and tonight a select and rare audience of one. Occasionally I find an exquisite treasure. Tonight you are that treasure."

"Treasure? Me? What is going on?"

"Don't you know yet?"

She looked away, searching for the answer. As if to defend herself from the impossible truth of this encounter, she stepped back and blurted, "Normally I would never come over to a stranger on a deserted beach in the middle of the night."

He countered, "Then why did you?"

"It was your voice. Your song called, no, compelled me. I didn't even think about it. I just did it."

Her words began to flow. "I'm inside, I'm out; I understand the mind of what you are singing about. I saw mermaids with big dark eyes and wavy hair . . . just like yours." She paused on the verge of another impossibility and shifted.

"Wait," she said, shaking her head. "I don't care how it works; it's like I have a new mind. All the grief I have felt for so long evaporated." She sputtered on, "I can't believe how happy I am. I may run down the beach and jump in the air!"

He grinned broadly. "I am here tonight for this, for you." He looked out toward the water, his hands gesturing seaward and back toward the island. "Some day I will compose a song for Hilton Head." With tenderness in his voice he stepped closer. "Your gift to me was a new composition, a song of healing. I experienced the pleasure of its birthing. You say my song called you, but your soul called me. That is the treasure we share."

He stepped closer and took her hand; and she felt something round, hard, and warm drop into it. He gently let go, and she saw in her palm a large, shimmering pearl. She drew a breath and opened her mouth to say something; but nothing came out. He took her other hand; and a flash of luminescence surrounded them for an instant, an alchemical mix of moonlight, pearl light, and something else, a blending of two spirits.

In that moment he brought her into his mind, and she knew him instantly. It became clear the beachcomber was not from this world but from someplace far more sacred and beautiful. There was no fear in that transcendent moment; there was simply a wordless recognition.

"Look. The tide has turned," he said. "Let's walk for a while."

They started down the beach in the direction of Mel's house. Their voices blended with the sound of soft, splashing waves as they spoke of the beauty of the night. Ghost crabs and sea foam scattered before them. A gentle, sensuous breeze played through her hair; the moon reflected a halo across his face.

When they reached Mel's house, she pointed the way to her door; and in a silent decision they walked up to the patio. She offered him a lounge chair and disappeared into the kitchen, returning with two glasses of wine. They sat and sipped. He sang and taught her some songs. She found her voice, and together they made music.

As night transformed into the dawn hours, the two found themselves in the bedroom, draped in each others arms, wrapped in the intensity of new-found love. As dawn streamed in through the open window, filtered by flowing curtains touching Aden's face, she looked deeply into his eyes and saw nothing but love reflected there.

"It's time for me to go now," he whispered.

"I know." She was completely at peace, and she knew why. The world called him, and distant shores awaited his song.

He kissed her. "There will be new songs to share with you, someday."

Standing on her balcony, she watched Aden walk into the ocean and dive beneath the waves. She laughed with a childlike joy, alone again but never again lonely, as she saw a large golden fish tail breach the calm, glassy surface with a big splash in the sparkling dawn.

She walked downstairs, and there on the chair was his guitar. Picking it up, she turned it over and saw on the back, scratched in big letters, "Beachcomber."

Mel also saw the vial of pills she had intended to take. She threw them into the garbage.

She set her pearl into a pendant and wore it always. The beachcomber had helped her discover love for the natural world. Her passion awakened, and she began to create art that expressed the deep awareness he had inspired in her. She learned to play his guitar and began singing and composing her own songs. Observing nature; walking in the wildlife preserve; watching dolphins hunt; studying seabirds, hawks, and herons—all became inspiration for her compositions. She studied art and began to work on canvas, attempting to capture the sway of the marsh grass, the giant thistle bushes, and sprawling vines that anchored themselves into the landscape of the dunes. Always listening for every sound, she composed poems as she walked the beach. Her new friends were the artists with whom she studied and sang. She was never lonely because she was always creating. Occasionally she thought of Aden, her muse; and she smiled. And she would feel a connection, not an attachment.

One evening she sat on her patio and watched the full moon floating over the ocean. She saw someone walk straight out of the water toward her house. Her heart began to race with anticipation as he stepped onto the patio. His figure was shadowed until he got closer. She saw the big, broad smile and the long, curly, wet locks.

"Aden!" she cried.

He smiled. "Ah, my treasure, I told you I would be back with new songs to sing."

The Busy People

by
Bobbi Hahn

They are everywhere these days:
The busy people with their
Cell phones,
PDA devices,
And laptop computers.
In the grocery store, hunched
Over the produce,
Cell phone in hand—
Important decisions about dinner!
At the mall, young ones stroll in packs,
Text messages alerting them
To dates or gossip
That can't wait
Until they return home.
In restrooms, even,
One hears cell phone conversations
From the stalls on either side,
Interrupted only by a flush.
In airports, businessmen perch
On uncomfortable seats
Or sprawl on the floor,
Balancing laptops with wireless connections,
Scrolling for the latest stock quote
Or updates from the office.
A small device, fitting in a palm,
Can maintain a calendar,
Locate a restaurant,
Or answer email.

Of course, the worst offenders
Are those who talk or text
While driving:
Distracting as well as dangerous.
When did *everything* become
So instantly important?
And whatever happened to
Taking time
To smell the roses?

Control

by
Art Cornell

Sometimes we seem
To be lurching toward
Something big—
Significant,
Life altering,
Not out of control—
Just out of our control.

Bouquet

by
Art Cornell

Fears are opportunities
Waiting to be conquered,
Adding victories,
Like flowers,
To our vase of life.

The World of Golf

by
Dee Merian

As they settled into retirement together, any mutual interests Stella and Leo ever shared had begun to fade away. While Leo filled his days playing golf and drinking beer with his male foursome at the Wagging Fishtail Country Club, Stella sat home reading books. Her new bridge friends had told her about the Bargain Box, a place to buy books for less than a dollar each.

Her most recent purchase was engrossing, but Stella did remember to put it aside long enough to place a pork roast in the oven. Leo arrived home later to smell the roast burning. Stella gave scant recognition to him when he entered the house. She sat in a corner of the living room intently reading her book. Leo, with his bloodshot eyes and beer breath, was becoming a boring interruption.

Her latest novel selection was set in Michigan, her home state. In the story, the beautiful anti-heroine was a 1970s hippy with children out of wedlock. She posed as a patriotic American college instructor influencing campus students to demonstrate against the Vietnam War. Stella was fascinated reading about the time two bombs were set to detonate inside an armed services induction center. These were different experiences compared to her own conservative lifestyle raising three children. When she heard

Leo's footsteps next to her chair, she glanced up from her book.

"Hi, honey. Is dinner ready?" It was after five o'clock, and Leo was hungry. A long day of golf and several beers always increased his appetite.

"It's in the oven. Help yourself." Stella gestured with her free hand and continued to read. She remained in the living room until late that evening reading a thick book that would take her several hours to finish.

A few days later, Leo came home with flowers. He placed them in a vase of water and carried them to the dining room. He set the table, adding candles and wine glasses. He had decided to surprise Stella with a special dinner of fresh scallops. He was weary of the overcooked food the past few nights and wanted a delicious meal.

Suddenly Stella entered the front door. "I'm exhausted!" she announced. "I did a lot of errands this afternoon. The groceries are in the car. Could you bring them in for me? I even stopped by the church to pray," she remarked casually while continuing to list all her other errands.

"That's nice," commented Leo, trying to seem interested. "May I ask what you are praying for now?" Stella always had some special concerns, usually about their adult children.

"A happy marriage," Stella announced with a stern look on her face.

Leo was stunned. He thought they had a happy marriage. What was going wrong? He forgot about the groceries in the car.

"Let's eat," Leo said, wanting to enjoy a meal without any burnt edges.

"The table looks beautiful," said Stella with a smile.

Leo beamed from the compliment and poured a rosé wine, Stella's favorite, into two stemmed glasses.

"Here's to us," they spoke in unison and clicked their glasses.

"Stella, we need to talk." Leo placed his glass on the table after another sip of wine. "I don't mind that you have bought a lot of clothes this past month. We're on a fixed budget. But if you want them, that's okay. I'm going to accept a part-time job. It's only a few hours in the morning five days a week."

At first Stella did not respond. She sat with her eyes on her lap looking at her hands.

"I think you've been feeling neglected in this new retirement arrangement," continued Leo. "Am I the only one who's enjoying it? Do you want to move back to Michigan?"

"Do you?" she asked.

"Well, not really. I don't miss the snow and icy, cold weather."

"I know," answered Stella. "You hated shoveling the driveway in the winter, maintaining the house, and mowing the lawn every summer. Here you play golf all year instead of a few weeks. But I do miss all our old friends and relatives."

"What do you want to do?" he asked.

Stella was quiet for a long time. Then she spoke. "Let's stay here awhile longer. Don't worry about all the clothes I bought. I returned them today."

She did not tell Leo they were resale clothes she purchased from St. Francis Thrift Shop. Purchasing unneeded clothes and books to read late into the night had become her main activity. She had been an executive's wife in Dearborn, Michigan, and had status supporting her husband socially. Now she was squeezed into another role, waiting alone all day for Leo to come home from the country club.

Stella decided to make a bargain with herself. She would stop self-indulging and pay more attention to her husband. Maybe then he would spend more time with her. They were not getting any younger. After forty-one years together, the remainder of time should not be spent in isolation from one another. She was not sure returning to Michigan would change anything.

"If you would just play golf a little less," announced Stella.

Leo did not reply. For the moment the idea seemed unthinkable.

They continued to eat dinner and talked about a drive to the Gulf Coast. Stella wanted to visit St. Petersburg and the big Naval Aviation Museum at the air station in Pensacola. Leo agreed that would be interesting.

They went to bed early. After they fell asleep, Stella heard a noise and awakened, sure someone was in the house.

"Leo, wake up! I think there's a burglar in our house. Leo?"

Half asleep, Leo turned over to face her. "What's wrong?"'

"There's a burglar in the house."

"No, there isn't. It's just the wind."

"What could he be stealing?" Stella asked out loud.

"We don't have anything valuable," grumbled Leo. "We gave everything to our kids before we left Michigan."

"The burglar doesn't know that."

"What do you want me to do? Go downstairs and help him hunt?" said an exasperated Leo.

"What about your new golf clubs?"

"They're in the trunk of the car. I have an early golf tournament tomorrow. Please, let me sleep. If anything is missing in the morning, call the police."

Hearing no more noises, Stella assumed that Leo had been right—it had only been the wind. Nonetheless, Stella lay awake looking at the ceiling. Nothing had changed. Leo was interested in his next golf game more than he was interested in her feelings.

"God," she whispered. "Remember what we talked about earlier today? Maybe we should renegotiate our understanding. This plan we talked about. Let's change it. What if I take lessons and learn to play golf?" She could hardly believe she would even consider the idea. She fell asleep waiting for an answer.

That next afternoon Leo came home to tell Stella he had placed second in the country club golf tournament. He won a gift certificate to use anytime during the next year in the pro shop.

"Could I use some of that money for golf lessons?" inquired Stella.

Leo was surprised by her request. "Well, I guess so." Leo remembered her remark about traveling more. Maybe if she played golf, he could avoid the long car drives. Stella was a good wife, but she became really bossy on long trips in the car.

Stella borrowed an old set of clubs from a friend and began taking lessons. First she practiced on the driving range and then on the golf course.

Her new instructor was impressed. He confided to Leo one night during a country club dance, "You should buy Stella a matched set of clubs. It will improve her game. She has a lot of talent."

"Really?" Leo replied. "What's going on with Stella?"

"Didn't you know? Stella is playing her first club competition with Sandra Fields."

"Isn't that the pretty woman who always scores in the high seventies?"

"Right," said the pro with a laugh. "They are a force to be reckoned with in the women's tournament."

The next morning during breakfast, Leo announced it was time to give back the borrowed golf clubs. He would buy Stella a new set.

"Do you really mean that?" Stella asked in surprise.

"Yes, I do. I'm really proud of you. It's time you look like the player you have become."

Entering the pro shop that morning, Stella moved immediately toward the golf rack. "I want these."

Leo choked looking at the price. They were the most expensive set.

"Are you sure these are the right clubs?"

"Oh, yes. These are the clubs Sandy always uses."

Leo examined a fabric bag he thought would be appropriate.

"Oh, no. I can't use that golf bag," said Stella. "I want this one over here." She pointed to an expensive leather bag.

"Why that one?"

"Sandy always uses that style of golf bag."

Leo had not expected to purchase such high-ticket items. "Oh, well, if it makes you happy," he told her. He reached for a box of golf balls.

Stella stopped him. "Not those golf balls. I want these."

"What's the difference?" asked Leo.

"Sandy only uses these golf balls."

In a grandiose gesture, Leo walked to the women's clothes rack. "I suppose you want a new golf outfit."

"Oh, no, not that outfit."

"Why not? It looks good to me. Isn't this your size?"

"Yes it is, but Sandy always wears that outfit."

Stella was thrilled Leo was showing so much interest in her game. Learning to play golf was making a difference in his attitude toward her. She had become an individual with talent. She was pleased her prayerful bargain had become so successful.

After Sandy and Stella had completed a championship golf year, Stella came home one evening to announce they were entered an amateur women's golf tournament in Georgia. She was very excited about their packaged tour.

Leo was stunned. "What about me? You're leaving me all alone?"

"Don't you want me to go?" asked Stella.

Leo stood in the middle of his living room looking at his ceiling. He did not know what to tell her. Would he be cooking all his meals and wondering what she was doing with her life? Later that same evening, while lying in bed as he listened to Stella breathing next to him, he began his own prayerful bargain.

Max

by
Bobbi Hahn

Dogs at the beach offer valuable life lessons for us lesser beings. It is marvelous to see their obvious happiness at being able to run free at full speed, their delight in the simple pleasure of chasing a stick or a seagull, their unabashed pleasure in just being *alive*. They demonstrate how to enjoy each day and every *moment* of that day, taking joy in the simple things, proving that the best things in life *are* free. Teaching that unconditional love is powerful . . . and magical, they show that communing with nature is nurturing as well as healing.

The last few mornings I have been fortunate to watch a particular dog at play. Max is a five-year-old golden retriever, and his *joie de vivre* is highly contagious. When he arrives on the sand, he dashes immediately into the surf for a quick dunk. Then he goes back to his male companion person, who removes his collar and rakish bandanna.

Eyes attentively on the man and the ball in his hand, Max watches for finger signals telling him to stay or sit. As soon as the man's arm is cocked to throw the ball, Max takes off like a rocket. He charges into the waves, leaping over the smaller ones and muscling his way through the larger ones that sometimes nearly upend him.

Max is so at ease in the water, as if it is his natural habitat; it makes me wonder if he is part fish . . . or dolphin. He continues on into the deeper water, swimming strongly to his target, sometimes obscured by the swells. On those rare occasions when he cannot find the ball, he looks back to shore where the man points in the appropriate direction. And off Max goes to claim his prize.

Dog and man continue this activity for fifteen or twenty minutes while I sit on a storage box and sip my coffee. Over and over the throwing and retrieving are repeated, with Max as enthusiastic on the last toss as he was on the first.

Sometimes, if the man is preoccupied chatting with his female companion or a passerby, Max will take the ball and, with a quick flip of his head, toss the ball for himself.

He takes particular joy in the birds frequenting the area. Whenever he spots them—usually flying some distance out and parallel to the beach—he plunges into the water, head high, eyes holding fast to the pelican or gull. If the bird happens to fly over shallow water or the sand, he is off down the beach in happy pursuit until the man whistles him back.

He is a welcoming committee of one, greeting each dog as it comes down the wooden walkway with its person close by. This morning he was joined by another golden, slightly larger than Max; they had the best time running together, frolicking in the water, tumbling in the sand.

His happiness is palpable. Everyone who passes by, walking or riding bikes, slows down or stops completely to watch him. And they smile. What a way to start the day!

Maple Creek Bridge

by
Sharon Rice

Swinging bridge at Maple Creek,
looking north to the swimming hole.
All my male cousins diving
into icy waters that shrivel the skin.
Their boy-man arms and legs careening
as they dare-devil each other into manhood.

Shamed, I walk south to the shallow pool
where I sit with my father,
our fingers trailing in the water,
watching the tiny shadow fish below.

Today in my head we are a wordless picture—
like the recently discovered photo from 1945
captured by the unblinking eye of a friendly voyeur
watching my young, smiling mama and
my tall, fearless daddy
standing side-by-side,
leaning over the terrible edge
of the swinging bridge.

Coffee Shop on Fourth Street

by
Sharon Rice

Today at the coffee shop on Fourth Street
you tell me you love me—
rather, that you loved me once.
The news draws in my breath, sharp and quick,
no space between the collision of theft and gift.

You say you laid down in the tall grass and cried
because you believed your only choice was not to.
As you say those words
I can hear your grief is gray and old;
mine is new and stinging green.

I sit, straight and still, across the table from you.
My fingers lace 'round the salt and pepper shakers.
A waitress bumps your elbow as she passes,
and I watch you brush the tea from your trousers
and hear you murmur something like, "I'm sorry."

(Published in *The Dark Woods I Cross*,
an anthology of women writers in Louisville, KY)

Love Affair at the Beach

by
Anne S. Grace

I believe each person is created with an identity to earth, wind, fire, or water. Nature draws us toward one element in particular. Mine is water; thus I enjoy ponds, lakes, creeks, rivers, and especially the ocean. The ocean air is full of healthy elements to breathe. I love the warmth of the sun kissing my skin. Watching the ocean waves crash or lap the shore and listening to the seagulls cry relaxes my taut mind and muscles. It is then I receive inspiration for writing articles, which I call my "Grace-By-the-Sea" stories.

Therefore, in December 1995 I set my course heading for Hilton Head Island, South Carolina. As soon as I arrived, I fell in love! When I crossed the bridges over the Intracoastal Waterway to the island, I felt at home. The island is a small, self-contained city, similar to a military base where I had lived previously, with all the same amenities from homes and shopping to social clubs and entertainment.

Each day on Hilton Head Island is a new adventure, like experiencing different lovers. I love watching the sand pipers run toward the water's edge and retreat when a wave crests. I am fascinated watching brown pelicans skim over the waves in formation, hunting for fish to eat. I love the feel of the warm water caressing my body when I take a dip.

Early one morning I saw several footprints in the sand of various beach creatures criss-crossed in a pattern. I added two of my own, and took a picture. We each share the same space on this planet.

Another day I encouraged a young boy visiting from a northern state, who closely examined things he found at the water's edge, to consider pursuing a career in aquaculture or oceanography when he is grown. I told him about my own son, who loved to hunt and fish, majoring in aquaculture at Texas A&M, getting a degree in Wildlife and Fisheries Science. The young boy and his mother appeared interested in considering the idea.

Once when my mother visited, we took a small lunch to eat at the beach that day. We had no idea there were so many seagulls on Hilton Head Island. One bird tried to snatch a sandwich from Mother's hand. We compromised by throwing corn chips in their direction. What fun! The little kid in both of us came out to play.

Another time I went to the beach on a sunny Sunday, a few days before the arrival of a hurricane. Blowing wind peppered my body with sand, like stinging pellets from a gun. As much as I love the beach, I did not stay long that day.

Each day when the tide turns I can sense that pregnant pause in the atmosphere. It is almost like time stands still for a moment. How exhilarating! But my favorite time at the beach is around five o'clock in the evening when the dolphins swim by on their way to Port Royal Sound. To me, it is a magical moment, knowing the day has almost ended.

When my husband retired and returned to the Lowcountry to live, we bought a house on the mainland, off Hilton Head Island. I no longer visit the beach regularly as I used to do. However, each time our children and grandchildren come, we make a fun trip to the beach.

The greatest thing about living near the ocean is the opportunity to experience it as often as I choose, No wonder I have a love affair each time I visit my beach.

The Bardo of Living and Dying

by
Margaret Lorine

That late January phone call changed my life.

"Rev. Dr. Winthrop is dead," said Madge Smythe, Cleveland University philosophy departmental secretary. "He passed away in the hospital this morning. Dean Burke is naming you his literary executor."

Shocked, I responded: "Edmund's dead? Why name me?"

"He left no will. You're his research assistant. Neither his bishop nor his relatives will challenge it; there's no payment involved."

Since receiving my Ph.D. in early December, I had been house-sitting for a friend's family on Hilton Head Island while editing Edmund's manuscript on *bardo*, the Buddhist experience of one's wandering between life and death. "I'm working on *The Bardo of Living and Dying*," I said, having accomplished little on it. Mostly I had been enjoying the island—walking the beach, breathing the fresh ocean air, and doing a bit of gardening for the Abercrombies.

"Come soon," Madge urged. "His church is arranging the funeral. Grad students are handling his classes for now." Emotion crept into Madge's voice. "It won't be the same without Dr. Winthrop."

"I'll pack and be there tomorrow."

"Michael Allen, a new student, told me Professor got really sick this time and went straight to the hospital, leaving his apartment a mess," Madge confided. "It's strange! Professor Winthrop only let his graduate assistant into his place. I thought he'd get Jenny Abercrombie to replace you, but he didn't."

"Jenny? But she's graduated."

"No, she didn't finish."

My head spun. I had agreed to house-sit while the Abercrombies went to France for Jenny's brother's wedding after graduation. Jenny, one of my closest friends, had not confided in me about her change of plans!

I tried not to think about Edmund or Jenny as I raced around her parents' ocean-front home packing. I called my former landlady, Heddy Simmons, for a room and caught the last flight from Savannah to Cleveland. Settled in as the plane's interior darkened, I allowed myself to think about Edmund.

Rev. Dr. Edmund Winthrop was a puzzle: single, eccentric, brilliant, charming, an Episcopal clergyman who taught atheistic existentialism. At fifty he cut a dashing figure in his high white collar and crisp black suit, with his shock of unruly golden hair, and his strong chin. A favorite guest on local television talk shows for his wit and worldly wisdom, his face and name were familiar to Clevelanders.

We celebrated Edmund's fiftieth birthday at Heddy's house just before my thesis defense. Heddy baked his favorite cake; the party was wonderful. He was overwhelmed. All his graduate students attended, except Jenny. She had phoned her regrets earlier: "Sorry, I'll be in Hilton Head packing for France."

Edmund brought Michael Allen, a visitor, who was looking at CU's Ph.D. program. The same Michael Madge said was in Edmund's apartment? Edmund did have a thing for boys, but he was too discreet to invite them home. Was Michael an exception? Maybe Edmund had come apart after I graduated.

At my dissertation defense, though Edmund knew my work thoroughly, he seemed unsure and unwell. The other examiners showed him solicitude. Students, especially the guys, admired him. Now his faculty competitors were helping him. Campus rumors hinted he was overworked; his drinking was getting to him; he had some unspecified ailment—but nothing fatal!

How could he be gone?

And Jennie in Cleveland? What about France?

As I leaned my forehead against the plane's darkened window, tears slid down my cheeks. A whiff of aftershave, a smoker's cough suggested that Edmund was not yet at rest. Uneasily, I dozed, half remembering something. What was it? Oh, yes—his directive in the *Bardo* manuscript: *Go to the Light. Do not be attached. Do not be distracted. Go straight to the Light.*

About 4:00 a.m. I trudged from the airport subway toward Heddy's porch light, bumping into a snow-shrouded garbage can. Hearing the crash, she opened the door before I knocked and welcomed me. We spoke tearfully of Edmund. Wanting to shake my eerie feelings, I confided: "I could feel his presence in the plane. Why he would want to haunt me? We had a working relationship; that was all." Going to my room, I felt creepy, as though he lurked nearby.

At eight o'clock I borrowed a coat and boots and took the subway to the university to see Madge. The Arts Tower elevator was locked. I would find Madge later. Edmund's apartment was across the quad, an easy walk even in snow. Its guard house was empty, but I still had my key. I let myself into #3C, Edmund's apartment, re-locking the door.

The place was deathly still with lingering odors of cigarette smoke and booze. Hercules was gone, his water dish empty; a dried-up can of cat food on the kitchenette floor. Somebody must have taken the cat days ago. In Edmund's study I checked on the damage. Expecting the worst, I was not disappointed. Amid piles of books and papers, there were cigarette butts, empty Scotch glasses, and remnants of cornbread, fried chicken, and collards. Edmund, a workaholic scholar and a strict vegetarian, never ate in his study. Cigarette stubs and empty drink glasses, yes; but chicken, no! And three plates? I slipped his daybook into my coat pocket from the pile of mess on his desk.

Overwhelmed and confused, I headed back only to find the campus closed due to snow. Walking toward Heddy's for time to think, I stopped by Freyvogel's Funeral Home to inquire if Professor Winthrop's body was there. Looking distraught and grief-stricken, Michael Allen answered the bell. He recognized me from Edmund's party and let me in.

"Michael, what are you doing here?"

"I'm an attendant," he said. "Edmund got me the job. He knows, I mean he knew, old man Freyvogel from his parish priest days. It's really weird. I can't believe it! I was working here just until he found me grant money for his program and now he's here—dead!"

"Michael, you poor thing! What are you going to do?"

"I don't know with my Professor gone!'"

"What happened to him?"

"I don't know. He'd get better; then he get sick again. With his heart and liver problems, the doctors said it was 'natural causes.' Do you want to see him? He's in the cooler."

"Would it be okay? Will you get into trouble?"

"Nobody's here. Ardith, the assistant, is stuck at home and the other guys are at a wreck. They're bringing in a family of three. With this storm, that'll take them a while."

I wasn't sure how I felt about this, but I wanted to say goodbye in relative privacy. In a room filled with tables and cabinets, Michael opened a drawer and pulled back the sheet. As Edmund's wavy, golden hair emerged, Michael began sobbing, head bowed, shoulders shaking.

I heard Michael murmur: "I can't believe I've lost you, just when we were getting so close, so in love."

Turning to me, Michael said: "Do you want a piece of his hair to remember him by? A lock from the back or side wouldn't be noticed."

Before I could answer, Michael fetched a pair of scissors lying nearby and snipped two tufts of hair. Sealing them in two envelopes, he gave me one and kept the other. I slid mine into the pocket of Heddy's coat beside the daybook. Offering a silent prayer for Edmund, I whispered to him to seek the Light. Then reeling from Michael's revelation of his love for Edmund, I hurried back to the main entrance and fled.

A blizzard was developing. I burrowed deeper into Heddy's warm coat and braced myself against the blowing gale. My eyelashes were sticking together as I approached "The Finishing Touch" where I had gotten my hair and nails done when I could afford it. It was open. Pat, my stylist, was alone, sipping coffee and leafing through an old issue of *Vogue*.

Seeing me enter, her face brightened. "Well, hello, stranger. What are you doing in Cleveland in the middle of a snowstorm? I thought you were off in paradise."

As I climbed into her chair for a long-overdue trim, I told her about Professor Winthrop. Pat was floored. Edmund was one of her regulars, though I was the only other person who knew he sneaked in regularly after hours for a shave, haircut, and dye job. The shave and cut were unremarkable, and no one suspected that his golden locks were anything less than the sign of his naturally enduring youth.

While Pat clipped and snipped, she described her new training in hair analysis. "I could do yours," she said, "as a welcome home gift."

"Could you test a piece of Edmund's hair, too?"

"What good would it do now? He won't be needing shampoo or conditioner."

"I know, but I have a feeling something's not right. You might discover something."

"I'm sure we'll find out his hair was dyed, and he smoked and drank too much."

"No, Pat," I said, "They said he died of 'natural causes,' but that's not it! Maybe, just maybe, you can find something out from his hair."

"I doubt it; but while I'm running yours, I could run his."

She took a lock of my cut hair, and I gave her some of Edmund's from my envelope. She did not ask where I got it. Labeling mine and his, she placed the hair samples in her processor and turned it on.

While Pat was doing my nails, I noticed a young woman walking past the salon's window. Our eyes met. She looked away and hurried on. I could have sworn it was Jenny Abercrombie, but this woman was pregnant. The wind pressed the front of her coat against her; I could see a distinct bulge. After she passed, I gaped at her back. It was Jenny, pregnant! How long had it been since I had seen her—two maybe three months?

"Pat," I gasped. "That was Jenny Abercrombie. She's pregnant!"

"Huh? She used to be a regular, but I haven't seen her in ages. A while back Edmund mentioned that Jenny was teaching him to 'eat Southern.'"

"You're kidding!"

"No. He told me he was tired of being a vegetarian—or was it a vegan—and eating out all the time. Anyway, he said Jenny had started cooking for him. Your nails are a mess. What have you been doing with your hands?"

"I weeded the Abercrombies' garden down at Hilton Head without gloves. Sorry!"

"Well, they're a fright. You soak them while I check the hair samples."

Returning with a puzzled look, Pat said, "Your hair tests just as I expected. You need more calcium and iron, like every female your age. But, besides the usual damage from years of bleaching, Edmund's tests positive for arsenic—and lots of it!"

"Arsenic? Are you sure?"

"As sure as I can be."

I was shocked. I had to notify the police. But first I needed to see if there was any arsenic at Edmund's. The only kind I knew of was used to kill ants in the garden at Hilton Head. I paid Pat and headed out. I stopped by the funeral home to tell Michael not to let anyone work on Edmund until I told the police about this.

The assistant, Ardith, opened Freyvogel's door. She told me that Michael got a call and left to meet somebody at Dr. Winthrop's apartment. She did not know when he would be back.

Nearing Edmund's apartment, I saw flashing blue lights. Yellow crime tape roped off his building. Recognizing the doorman, I asked, "What's going on?"

"Oh, it's you, P. J." he said. "A resident found a young man's foot sticking out of a third floor doorway and called the police. He thought the victim was a visitor, not a tenant. The police are searching the building now. If I could get up there, I could probably identify him."

I feared it was Michael. Wanting to talk to Heddy before calling the police, I walked quickly to the university subway. The platform was nearly deserted. I stood just inside the entrance between two benches where men in dirty jeans and ripped jackets were dozing. As the train approached, I heard the outside door open behind me and felt a blast of cold air. Someone hit me in the back and shoved me toward the oncoming train. At that moment one of the drunken men got up from his bench and lurched into me. I grabbed him. Together, we fell backward away from the on-coming train.

The drunk saved my life. As we picked ourselves up, my attacker retreated through the station door. But I managed to glimpse her back.

It was a back I recognized.

While I pressed some coins of gratitude into my savior's hands, the train pulled to an abrupt stop. The engineer declared an emergency, locked the train's doors shut and hurried over to me.

"Are you okay? I never could've stopped in time. Even if I had, you could have landed on that third rail, and you'd have been a goner. Please come with me. My passengers will have to wait."

Shaken, I followed him into a tiny control room. I sat on the only chair while he called the police. An apparent veteran of such occurrences, he had stopped all trains entering this station, gotten my information, and written up his eyewitness account before the police arrived.

Two officers pulled up through the university parking garage, sirens blaring. They took the engineer's report, hustled me into their waiting cruiser, and whisked me off to the division precinct. Feeling like a felon, I asked if I could make one call.

Heddy's place was just across the Cuyahoga River. She said she would come by taxi immediately. Sitting alone drinking the world's strongest coffee, I could hear the police radio in the background. The body found in University Gardens #3C was that of an unidentified male. It was believed he was hit on the head by someone inside the apartment as he opened its door. There was no suspect or motive. It was thought that the perpetrator left some evidence at the crime scene.

I swallowed hard. The victim had to be Michael. But who killed him and why? He was distraught at Edmund's death. Certainly he had nothing to do with it, nor did he suspect the death as unnatural.

Heddy bustled in and grabbed me. I began to cry.

"There, there, honey," she soothed. "It's going to be okay. You're safe now. The police will figure all of this out."

Somebody led us to a conference room. Sheriff Otis Grimes came in, introduced himself and Kyle Cardman from the district attorney's office, and placed a tape recorder on the table for my statement.

"Now, ma'am," the sheriff opened, "please tell us exactly what happened in the subway station."

"I think there's more to this, not just the attack on me," I asserted. Clenching Heddy's hand, I described my visit to Dr. Winthrop's apartment, the uncharacteristic food leftovers, and the absence of the cat. I told him about meeting Michael Allen at Freyvogel's Funeral Home. "I think he was killed today in the Professor's apartment," I added.

"Why so?" Mr. Cardman probed, taking notes.

"Because the funeral home assistant said someone called and asked Michael to come to Dr. Winthrop's apartment."

"Why would someone want to kill him?"

"I don't know. He was new in Cleveland, a friend of the Professor's." I had no idea how Michael's revelation that morning that he loved Edmund might play into the drama. But I kept quiet out of respect for Edmund's personal life, of which I had gathered only a few hints over the years I had known him.

"The death certificate says Dr. Winthrop died of

natural causes. Why do you think he was murdered?" Mr. Cardman asked, his black eyes steady on my face.

"I took the hair sample . . . "

"The what?"

I was getting in deep. I relayed how Michael clipped some hair from the corpse and how I gave it to a beautician to analyze. I felt foolish, but the police needed to know about the arsenic. I handed my envelope across the table. The sheriff opened it, studied the curly golden lock a moment, and rebuked me.

"You should have brought this straight to us, ma'am."

"Yes, but first, I wanted to check Dr. Winthrop's apartment for arsenic and tell Michael not to let anyone work on the Professor's body."

"So you tried to warn Michael Allen. Then what happened?"

"I went to the apartment, but the place was cordoned off. The doorman said a young man was found dead—murdered! I just wanted to go home to Heddy to decide what to do."

"Any thoughts on who your subway perpetrator might be?"

Words stuck in my throat. It was hard to accuse my close friend of trying to kill me.

Heddy squeezed my hand. "Hon, tell him. You aren't safe 'til this is over."

"Jenny Abercrombie. I recognized her coat. It's red, brown, and orange, kind of mottled-looking. She had it on this morning when I saw her out the beauty salon window."

"Why would Ms. Abercrombie want to kill you?"

I shook my head. "I don't know."

"Do you think she murdered Michael Allen?"

My head beginning to throb, I replied, "I don't know."

"If Dr. Winthrop was murdered—and I say 'if'—do you think Mr. Allen or Ms. Abercrombie did it?"

"No."

I chewed my lip. "Not Michael Allen. No! But I don't know about Jenny Abercrombie. Maybe. Why should she attack me if she didn't?"

He countered, "Why would she attack you if she did?"

"She could have thought we knew something—that we were a threat. Maybe she did kill Michael; then she tried to kill me."

Mr. Cardman stood up. "We'll test this hair sample to see if the Professor was poisoned, as you suggest. You'll need to identify the murder victim. We'll collect samples from the food and from the cat food. You say the cat is missing?"

"He wasn't there. The doorman might know if someone took him."

"We'll check," he said.

At the morgue I identified Michael Allen. He lay on a table. Dried blood from the gash in his skull clung to his face, and a blank tag hung from his big toe. The room stank of chemicals. I was grateful to return to Mr. Cardman's office.

"Found this at the scene," he said, "caught in Mr. Allen's hair."

He produced a broken charm, a handcrafted lighthouse from Hilton Head. I told him I had seen Jenny wearing a similar one.

"The sheriff's sending you home in a squad car and posting a guard on the house tonight. Patrols will look for Jenny Abercrombie," Mr. Cardman said.

Once home, we dead-bolted the door. Heddy collapsed exhausted on the parlor daybed. From the coat pocket I retrieved Edmund's daybook and snuggled close by Heddy in a comfortable chair. I mused and wept as I turned pages that recorded mundane events—some of which involved me—library books needed or due back, lecture subjects to work up, meeting reminders, dinner dates, even a note to pick up papers from me at Heddy's the night of his party. When I finally closed the book, a folded onionskin paper with Edmund's minute scrawl fell from between the cover and binding.

I read in fascinated horror: *"Jenny has gotten herself pregnant. It will never work. I envisioned a divine 'ménage a trois'—I the Father, Michael the Son, and Jenny the Spirit, the female principle that holds us together. But no, that little vixen had to go and ruin it. I told her to get an abortion; she won't. Her money can't buy me. I'll never marry her. That would end everything I enjoy with the boys. Now, Michael, he is perfect; but we have to replace Jenny. I have told her to take Hercules, who has grown attached to her, and get out of the apartment and out of our lives! Did I make a mistake in not trying P.J. for the part?"*

I was overcome with shock and disbelief. How could I have worked so closely with the Professor, never suspecting his dark intent to involve a male student acquaintance and my own best friend in his sordid drama!

Edmund's work on the *bardo*, the experience of a person wandering, lost between life and death, had perhaps a desperate personal meaning for him that I had not seen. My urgings of Edmund since his death: "Do not be attached or distracted. Go to the Light!" now took on a note of desperation—for both of us! From the depths of my depression, a sense of peace that I had escaped struggled to emerge. I yearned for the innocence of my graduate studies, the beauty of Hilton Head's ocean; but reality pulled me back. I took a deep breath and dialed Mr. Cardman.

Nearly three months have passed. While his church, the university, and the community at large memorialized the image of the Rev. Dr. Edmund Winthrop that they had known and loved, Mr. Cardman continued his investigation. He managed to keep it and the note on the onionskin paper out of the news until sometime after the Professor was buried. The search for Jenny Abercrombie has turned up nothing so far.

Still feeling the lack of resolve, I nonetheless accepted a position as visiting assistant professor at CU and took up residence at Heddy's place.

This day I sat, staring out the window of Edmund's former office on a break from correcting exams. On the desk Edmund's *The Bardo of Living and Dying* manuscript lay completed. On the title page, below *Edmund F. Winthrop, D.D., Ph.D.*, I placed my name, Penelope Joan Thistle, Ph.D., editor.

The phone's ring startled me. I answered, "Dr.

Penelope Thistle."

"This is Kyle Cardman. The river patrol pulled a body out of the thawing Cuyahoga. It may be Jenny Abercrombie. Sorry to ask, but I'd like your preliminary I.D. before we call her parents in South Carolina."

"Can Heddy come along? She needs some closure. She's still taking this pretty hard, though I think she's enjoying my new job nearly as much as I am!"

He chuckled. "I look forward to seeing you both."

Closure. Heddy wasn't the only one who needed it.

About the Contributors

James Edward Alexander, Esq., a native of Valdosta, Georgia, shares memories of his happy childhood in his book, *Half Way Home from Kinderlou*. His latest publication is *If I Should Die Before I Wake . . . What Happens to My Stuff?* Although he still maintains a law office in California, he lives in Bluffton, South Carolina, where he continues to write about the exciting and varied experiences during twenty years of active duty in the Air Force.

Jane Anderson is a self-taught artist living on Hilton Head Island. She is a member of the Hilton Head Art League. She loves to paint pictures of animals and birds and particularly enjoys creating greeting cards for her five children, their spouses, and her twelve grandchildren. Her art work can be viewed and purchased at the Art League Gallery in The Pineland Station Mall.

Will Anderson earned a doctoral degree from MIT, served as an army Captain, and spent twenty-nine years with NASA as an engineer and senior executive. He has written two techno-thriller novels: *The Backdoor* and *The Anomaly*. (Preview on *www.willandersonauthor.com*). He drew on his knowledge of aerospace systems, piloting and related experiences, relationships, and travels to write these exciting, believable novels.

A native of Roanoke, Alabama, **Fred Bassett** is an award-winning poet and Biblical scholar who holds four academic degrees, including a Ph.D. in Biblical Literature from Emory University. His poems have been published in more than fifty journals and anthologies. Paraclete Press has published two books of "found" poetry that he created from Biblical lyrics—*Love: The Song of Songs* and *Awake My Heart: Psalms for Life*.

Iowa natives, **Roger and Linda Benning** lived in California, North Carolina, and New Jersey prior to following their long time friends, Sansing and Terry McPherson, to a dream retirement on Hilton Head Island. Both enjoy photographing the wonderful sights in the Lowcountry as well as their five beautiful grandchildren.

Raymond P. Berberian is an attorney living in Beaufort County, South Carolina. He is a graduate of New York University with a B.S. degree in economics and a graduate of St. John's University Law School with J.D. degree. Originally from New Jersey, he practiced law in New Jersey and New York for over thirty-five years before relocating to Hilton Head Island.

Len Camarda earned his B.S. and M.B.A. degrees from St. John's University in New York. He spent a forty-year career in the pharmaceutical industry, much of that time working internationally and living overseas in Panama, Holland, and Spain. His passion for art and creative writing moved to a higher level with his retirement in 2003. He exhibits his oil paintings regularly at the Art League Gallery in Pineland Station and has completed a novel, *The Seventh Treasure*, which he plans to publish.

Art Cornell, an acclaimed photographer, poet, and painter of abstract art, has been creating images and poetry for nearly forty years. His poetry books *In the Wind*, *Heart Rhythms*, and *Riding on a Rainbow* incorporate his black-and-white photographs. His paintings and photography can be viewed at the Hilton Head Art League, Calhoun Street Art Gallery, Pink House Art Gallery, and at his website: www.artbyartcornell.com. His art resides in private and corporate collections throughout the United States.

A native of Whitinsville, Massachusetts, **Tom Crawford** graduated from Westminster College in New Wilmington, Pennsylvania, and studied at the University of Munich. He began his career as a reporter with *The Worcester Telegram*; worked in the Springfield (Massachusetts), Boston, London, and Belgrade bureaus of United Press

International; and returned to Springfield as copy and news editor of *The Springfield Union* and *Sunday Republican*. He has published *Foibles, a* collection of vignettes; and he is readying a completed memoir, *Resurrections . . . of an Obituary Writer*, and a novel, *Goli Otok* (Naked Island), for publication.

Originally from North Wales, **Sheila Gale** immigrated to Canada and worked as a college professor for twenty-eight years, teaching supervisory management and creative writing. Since retiring seven years ago, she and her husband, Ted, spend winters on Hilton Head Island enjoying cycling around the island, walking on the beach, and socializing with the many friends they have made here, both Canadian and American. Now pursuing a writing career, she is working on her third novel.

Anne S. Grace is known as a Christian Communicator. Through Gift of Grace Ministries, she writes articles of Inspiration/Education at www.giftofgrace.injesus.com. She has authored two books: *GRACE UPON GRACE*, her journey of faith, and a devotional, "The ABC's of Grace." She is a native Virginian and graduate of Radford University, A former elementary teacher, she has four grown children and eight grandchildren. Anne and her husband reside in Bluffton, South Carolina.

Bobbi Hahn's poetry has been published in several anthologies; her essays have appeared online and in various newsletters. Her "day jobs" have included: travel agent, community theater general manager, commercial insurance agent, and art gallery director. Bobbi, her husband, and two lazy cats began visiting Hilton Head to escape Ohio winters. During the fourth such visit, they decided to stay. Forever. They have lived here since 2004. She is working on a novel.

Bob Hamel is retired and has been living on Hilton Head for ten years. He is a graduate of Pace University, Lubin School of Business, New York City, with a BBA and three years of graduate studies. Literature is his real love with published poetry books, *Reflections of Time* and *Night is Falling*. He volunteers weekly teaching Creative Writing to fifth grade students and reading poetry to seniors at retirement homes.

With degrees from the University of South Carolina, Georgia Institute of Technology, and Georgia State University, **Jane Hill** has published numerous technical works in the U. S., Canada, and Europe. A native South Carolinian, she is now writing about the Lowcountry, where she spent many happy childhood vacations. Her recent works include two young adult novels, *Clarendon Island* and *Only a Ghost of a Chance*, published by Salt Marsh Cottage Books, www.smc-books.com.

Ann Judge-Wegener's artistic work has been accomplished in pencil, pen and ink, chalk, and oil. Her artistic talent became evident when she was a child and was nurtured during her high school days through art lessons. Following graduation from Purdue University, she devoted much of her artistic efforts to the drawing and painting of animals, particularly horses. She is an accomplished horse trainer and international horse judge. She is known to Denver Broncos football fans as the "Bronco Girl" who rides Thunder, the Broncos mascot, at each home game.

Having grown up in Indiana, **Max Judge** is Professor Emeritus of Animal Sciences from Purdue University. He has published books entitled *Chronicles of Life in the Midwest*, a depiction of rural life during the decade of the 1940s; and *The Bronco Girl*, an account of his daughter's horse-related career including riding Thunder, the Denver Broncos mascot. Both books are published by Salt Marsh Cottage Books (www.smc-books.com). His writing is an extension and revision of his professional career as author or coauthor of scientific publications, research abstracts, and textbooks.

Norm Levy retired as Director, Advertising Development, of Procter & Gamble and moved to Hilton Head Island in 2004. He is a published song writer (Blues and Country &

Western)—sorry, no hits. He writes mostly topical light verse, but the Lowcountry's natural beauty has inspired a more lyrical exploration. Norm has a book nearing publication: *Rhymes For Our Times (Skews on the News)*.

Marilyn Lorenz has been writing since she was in third grade, when her teacher encouraged her to read her stories for "show and tell." A Creative Writing Graduate of Northwestern University, she has previously published poetry, short stories, lyrics, and music. Marilyn's children's picture book, *Great Blue Gert*, published through a Grant from the National Endowment for the Arts and the Arts Council of Beaufort County, sold out in 2008.

Margaret Lorine (aka Lorine M. Getz, Ph.D.), Moderator of the Island Writers' Network (IWN), conceived and guided IWN's first joint writing project, *Hilton Head Island: Unpacked & Staying*. She also served as one of the editors of *Hilton Headings*. A member of the Queen's Writers Group and the North Carolina Writers' Workshop, and for many years a university professor of Art, Literature, and Religion, she has authored numerous works of fiction and non-fiction. Best known for her volumes of Flannery O'Connor, she co-edited *The Kissing Bough* with Judith Simpson. Her short story, "Bardo Winter," has been published in *Tales for a Long Winter's Night*.

Charlie McOuat is a retired dentist from Cape Cod. He has published articles for United Planet about his volunteer experiences in Africa. He has also published articles in *Hilton Head Monthly* about his tutoring English at Literacy Volunteers of the Lowcountry. He continues his quest for youth by rowing with the Palmetto Rowing Club and by drinking moderate amounts of red wine with his wife and friends.

Sansing McPherson, an Alabama native, graduated from Auburn University, holds an MEd from Kean University of New Jersey, and taught English and writing from elementary through college level. After twenty-five years in New Jersey she and her husband returned to the South to retire on Hilton Head Island. She has been a staff writer for *101 Things to Do on Hilton Head*, is a free-lance editor, and writes short stories and novels.

Dee Merian, a native of Santa Monica, California, holds a Master's degree from New York University and a Writers Certificate from Iowa University. She has lived on Hilton Head Island with her husband John for ten years. A former airline hostess, nurse, dietician, college professor, and award-winning story teller, she has published four books: *American Mosaic*, *Counterfeit Horserace*, *Flying High*, and *Southern California Stories*.

Shanti North is a parent, traveler, teacher, and veteran of life's experience. From this perspective she hopes to express some of the deep-seated lessons, concepts, and valuable insights into the ongoing mystery of life. With a keen interest in the natural world and a wish to illuminate the fullness of its inherent value, her writing is laced with elements of the philosophical, the sensory, and the mystical. She has been published in magazines and collected works.

A native of southern Ohio, **Sharon Rice** has studied abroad through the generous funding of the Grawemeyer Foundation, sung in opera choruses, played Dorothy in Miller's *After the Fall*, and published works in several religious journals. Jim Wayne Miller awarded her poem "Solitude" third place in his national contest, and "The Coffee Shop on Fourth Street" appeared in the anthology of contemporary Louisville women poets, *The Dark Woods I Cross* (1992).

David Russell, graphic designer, moved to the Hilton Head/Bluffton area in 2001 from New York where he did ads, logos, brochures, catalogs, magazines, signage, and package design for many clients, including projects for IBM and Bloomingdales. His book design work includes art direction, layout, and cover design for Peachtree Publishers, Ltd.; Franklin Library, a division of the Franklin Mint; and

Time/Life's "Wild Wild World of Animals." Check out David's talent at www.davidrusselldesigns.com.

Originally from the Buffalo, New York, area, **Greg Smorol** is a retired efficiency consultant who operated a business throughout the South for many years. He received his Baccalaureate Degree from St. Lawrence University in Canton, New York, and a Masters Degree in Communications from SUNY at Buffalo. He enjoys writing poems and short stories as well as novels. He and his wife Donna currently reside on Hilton Head Island.

Charlie Thorn served in Army Intelligence before enrolling at NYU. After a year he transferred to Northwestern's Medill School of Journalism. He began his publishing career at the *Daily News*, moving on to *Newsweek*, and then *Forbes* in New York and Atlanta. Semi-retired, Charlie conducts historical tours of enigmatic Daufuskie Island and recently completed his first novel. Originally from New York State, he has lived on Hilton Head Island with his wife, Carole, since 1986.

Norma Van Amberg, editor of *Coastal Sport and Wellness*, is an award-winning journalist who wrote for various papers in her native New Jersey as well as for the Hilton Head *Island Packet*. She has lived in the Hilton Head area since 1984 and is an avid sports and outdoors enthusiast.

Jim Van Cleave retired as Vice President, Media and Programming, from Procter & Gamble. He is active in Lifelong Learning of Hilton Head Island where he teaches courses and writes the organization's ads and catalogs. He amuses himself, family, and friends writing short stories, most of which are pure fiction . . . but some are not.

Island Writers' Network of Hilton Head Island

As the title of this volume implies, members of the Island Writers' Network have headed to Hilton Head Island from all over the map. Though their backgrounds are diverse, they share a common passion for writing.

The Island Writers' Network aims to support, inspire, and mentor writers in both the business and the craft of writing. Members write in all genres, including fiction, nonfiction, memoir, children's literature, and poetry. They range in experience from the aspiring neophyte to the multi-published author.

The organization was founded in 1999 by Jo Williams with eighteen members at its first meeting. As the membership grew, the group helped launch the careers of several charter members. Notable alumnae of IWN are Kathryn Wall, the author of nine Bay Tanner mysteries for St. Martin's Press; Vicky Hunnings, who has three mysteries published by Avalon Press; and Jo Williams, with a novel published by Coastal Villages Press. Many additional members have had the satisfaction of seeing their work in print through professional journals, magazines, anthologies, and various self-publishing avenues.

In 2007 IWN published its first anthology, *Hilton Head Island: Unpacked & Staying*, which sold nearly a thousand copies. That volume and this new one have given members hands-on experience with the publishing process from developing the germ of an idea, through writing and revision, all the way to the selection of a publisher and marketing the finished product.

Both IWN anthologies, *Hilton Headings* and *Hilton Head Island: Unpacked and Staying*, are available at numerous locations in the greater Hilton Head area. For a current list of vendor outlets and instructions for on-line ordering, please visit the IWN website at www.iwn-hhi.org.

IWN meets on the first Monday of each month at 7:00 p.m. in the Heritage Library on Hilton Head Island. Visitors and new members are always welcome, regardless of writing experience.

Also by the
Island Writers' Network of
Hilton Head Island

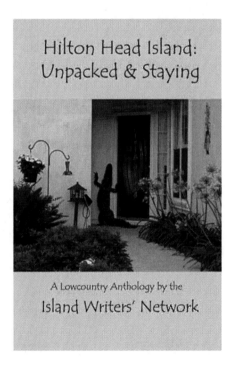

The Island Writers' Network's first anthology, *Hilton Head Island: Unpacked & Staying*, has sold nearly a thousand copies since its publication in 2007. While its forty-plus entries vary from light humor to deep spirituality, each conveys the writer's intense love of the island that we are so fortunate to call home.

David Lauderdale of *The Island Packet* called it ". . . an impressive new Lowcountry anthology." *Hilton Head Monthly* said the anthology shows "what an amazing variety of talents can be found in this outstanding coalition of area writers."

Hilton Head Island: Unpacked and Staying is still available for sale at outlets in the greater Hilton Head area. Please see the IWN web page—www.iwn-hhi.org—for the latest list of vendors.

Index of Authors

Alexander, James Edward 1, 71, 145
Anderson, Will 37
Bassett, Frederick W. 34, 90, 116, 129, 142
Berberian, Raymond P. 25
Camarda, Len 49
Cornell, Art 42, 91, 130, 141, 174
Crawford, Tom 3, 159
Gale, Sheila 83
Grace, Anne S. 185
Hahn, Bobbi 43, 127, 172, 181
Hamel, Robert 35, 48, 150
Judge, Max D. 21, 81
Levy, Norm 33, 70, 92, 118
Lorenz, Marilyn 20, 60, 126, 144, 158
Lorine, Margaret 187
McOuat, Charlie 61, 95
McPherson, Sansing 7
Merian, Dee 175
North, Shanti 163
Rice, Sharon 19, 82, 94, 119, 148, 183, 184
Smorol, Greg 46, 65, 151
Thorn, C. S., Jr. 107
Van Amberg, Norma 77
Van Cleave, Jim 131

Index of
Photographers and Illustrators

Anderson, Jane...36
Benning, Linda..102
Benning, Roger..105
Cornell, Art............................19, 35, 100, 104, 141
Crawford, Phyllis...161
Hahn, Bobbi...76, 162
Hill, Jane..64, 91, 174
Judge-Wegener, Ann..81
McPherson, Sansing..........6, 24, 99, 101, 103, 106, 158
Van Amberg, Norma...80